Kildee House

Other Books in the Newbery Honor Roll Series

Chúcaro: Wild Pony of the Pampa
Francis Kalnay

The Defender
Nicholas Kalashnikoff

The Great Wheel
Robert Lawson

Mountain Born
Elizabeth Yates

The Moved-Outers
Florence Crannell Means

Old Ramon
Jack Schaefer

•THE•NEWBERY•HONOR•ROLL•

Kildee House

Rutherford Montgomery

Illustrations by Barbara Cooney

Walker and Company
New York

TO McCLOY

This edition published in the United States of America in 1993 by Walker Publishing Company, Inc.

Published simultaneously in Canada by Thomas Allen & Son Canada, Limited, Markham, Ontario

Library of Congress Catalog Card Number: 93-15624

Printed in the United States of America

1 2 3 4 5 6 7 8 9 10

Kildee House

CHAPTER ONE

JEROME KILDEE had built himself a house on the mountainside. It was an odd house because Jerome Kildee was an odd man. He built his house under a giant redwood tree on Windy Point. Since the days of Julius Caesar creatures had been building homes at the foot of the redwood or in its branches. At the time Jerome built his house most folks did not build on knobs high on a mountainside, even the round-topped, wooded mountains of the Pacific Coast Range.

What the neighbors said or what they thought was of no concern to Jerome. The day he walked out on Windy Point, and looked up at the giant redwood towering into the sky, and stood savoring the deep silence, he knew he was going to stay. When he turned from the great tree and looked down over the green ridges, the smoky valley, into the gray-white haze of the Pacific, he smiled. This was a land of silence, the place for a silent man.

The house Jerome built was not as wide as the redwood; to have made it so wide would have been a waste of space, because Jerome did not need that much room. He toted the biggest window he could buy to the cabin, and set it in the wall which faced a panorama of ridges and valleys. The window was as high as the wall; it was one wall as far across as the door. It had been rolled out as a plate-glass window for a store.

The back wall was the redwood trunk. It made an odd house, one wall curved inward, and finished with shaggy redwood bark. Jerome rented a horse and packed Monterey stone up for a fireplace. The fireplace was a thing of beauty. It filled one end of the room. The cream Monterey stone, traced through with threads of red, was carefully fitted and matched for grain; the hearth was wide, and the mantel was inlaid with chips of abalone shell. It was the last piece of stonework Jerome planned to make, and he made it a masterpiece. In a recess back of the last slab of stone he tucked away the tools of his trade and sealed them into the wall. Jerome Kildee, maker of fine monuments, was no more. There remained only Jerome Kildee, philosopher, a silent little man, seeking to become a part of a silent mountain.

Jerome Kildee did not work. He owned the hundred acres of woods and hillside around him, but he did not clear any of it. He bought all of his food, and he had stove and fireplace wood hauled up and stacked outside his door. Jerome hired the Eppys to haul the wood to the bottom of the hill, then up the hill with their tractor because there was only a winding footpath up from his mailbox. The Eppys laughed and made quite a bit of it. Jerome had hundreds of cords of oak and madroña close to his cabin. The farmer and his sons would have cut it and sawed it for a tenth of what Jerome paid for the wood and the hauling.

Jerome had no near neighbors, nor would he ever have any, because he had built in the exact center of his hundred acres. He had gone through life silent, unable

to talk to people, expecting them to leave him to his own thoughts. He had never visited the Eppy family after they hauled his wood, although they lived at the foot of his hill on the north side. They put him down as a queer one. The nine Eppys, as they were known locally, were robust folks. The six sons were all over six feet tall. Emma Lou would someday be almost as tall as her brothers. The Cabot place, at the foot of the mountain on the other side of the hill, was certainly not a place where Jerome would care to go. It was a fine estate with landscaped gardens and a swimming pool. The Cabots had one son, Donald Roger, who had never given Jerome more than a brief look.

But Jerome Kildee found he was not without friends. He had a host of friends and he didn't have to talk to them to keep their friendship. In fact, his silence helped to keep them friendly. They were all interested in him, a new experience for Jerome, and he was interested in them. Jerome found that they were not unlike the people back where he had operated his monument shop. They were willing to take advantage of him, they were selfish, and some of them were thieves, like the trade rats who packed off anything they could carry, regardless of whether or not they could use it. He soon learned that none of the raccoons could be trusted inside the cabin. They unscrewed the caps off ketchup bottles as easily as he could do it; they unlatched cupboard doors or opened them if there was a knob on them. One old raccoon, who was the neighborhood grouch, lived in a hole in the trunk of his redwood tree. Old Grouch had refused to move when Jerome built his house. He considered the redwood tree his tree. He made it clear to Jerome that he was trespassing.

The pair of spotted skunks who set up housekeeping under his floor were folks of a different sort from the raccoons. They were not dull-witted stinkers of the sort Jerome had known in his boyhood, dumb fellows who for ages had been depending upon poison gas instead of their wits for protection. They carried guns but seldom used them. The little spotted skunks were as smart as the raccoons, and about as curious. They had a real sense of humor and were always playing pranks on the raccoons. With them around, Jerome always had to get down on his hands and knees and explore the chimney of his fireplace before he built a fire. The skunks liked the fireplace and would gladly have traded it for their nest under the floor. They were not big stinkers like the swamp skunks, so Jerome could always fish them out of the chimney with his broom.

Jerome would probably have been crowded out of his house by the assortment of mice that found his house and the fine bark wall of the redwood to their liking if it had not been for the spotted skunks. The skunks had large appetites, so they kept the mouse population on an even keel. Two big wood mice lived in a bark nest back of a knot in the tree trunk. They furnished dinners for the spotted skunks with a regularity which should have become monotonous. How they could go on having big families, nursing them to a size to go out into the world, only to have them gobbled up one at a time as they left the nest, was more than Jerome could understand.

There was another pair of mice who lived under his bed in a box of old letters, which they made good use of without snooping into the contents, or trying to figure out why Jerome had tied them in bundles. They chewed up all of the letters except those written in indelible pencil. This removed from Jerome's life any desire to brood over the past. The spotted skunks could not get into the box. The mice went in through a knothole in the end. But their families suffered the same fate as the wood mice. And they went on having big families.

Jerome's wooded acres harbored many black-tailed deer and many gray foxes and possums. The foxes never made friends, and the possums ignored him because he never kept chickens. They had no bump of curiosity to draw them to his house. He saw them often and had a nodding acquaintance with them, so to speak. The black-tails visited his garbage pit regularly. The does often brought their fawns into his yard. But they did not bother much with him because he did not grow a garden or set out young fruit trees. He was about like any other dweller on the wooded mountain: he just lived there.

It was during the second year that Old Grouch turned the head of a dainty little miss. She was just sixteen months old, and like many another lass before her, she fell in love with a good-for-nothing. Old Grouch brought her to his nest in the redwood. It was high up on the tree where a burl formed a deep pocket. Old Grouch had learned that a redwood tree was a safe haven. When coon dogs chased him, followed by yelling humans, all he had to do was shinny up the giant tree. The hunters could not shake him out or climb the tree. Of course after Jerome came, the coon dogs and the hunters stayed away.

Old Grouch brought his bride home in January during the heavy rains. In April she presented him with a family. Like many another good-for-nothing, Old Grouch failed to provide for his family, though he did share the nest with them, taking the dry side and grabbing any of the food she rustled which suited his taste. Jerome couldn't climb the tree to look into the nest, but he heard the babies and listened to the family chitchat over them.

Old Grouch mildly irritated Jerome. He was smug

and fat, always ready to march into the cabin and demand part of Jerome's fried egg or lamb chop, but never thanking his host for anything, and always staying outside unless there was food. Any friendly advance was always met with a snarl or a snapping of white fangs. He was a surly fellow, but Jerome admired the way he had with the ladies.

His wife was of a different sort. She was friendly and thankful to Jerome for bits of food he gave her. She visited the cabin while he was in it, and not just when it was mealtime. She would have taken over his larder if he had allowed it. Her willingness to shift Old Grouch's responsibility for the family to him gave Jerome a problem. He was forced to invent new catches for his cupboard doors, and to fashion latches for his pull drawers.

Outwitting the slim little bride was no easy matter. With feminine wile she made up to Jerome, letting him stroke her head and scratch around her ears, smiling coyly up at him as he sat in his padded chair, but raiding his cupboard as sure as he went for a walk. Jerome fixed inside catches for the doors worked by wires which went up through the inside of the cupboard and were pulled by strings dangling from the ceiling, well out of reach of a raccoon. The pull drawers became pop-out drawers worked by wires with dangling strings attached to them.

CHAPTER ONE

Jerome's house was well decorated with strings hanging from the ceiling. A large button dangled at the end of each string like a black spider.

When Jerome wanted an egg for breakfast he pulled a string, and open popped a drawer exposing the egg carton. Then Jerome always had to take out two eggs because the minute the door popped open in popped Mrs. Grouch, and Jerome had to split fifty-fifty with her. He could have closed and barred the door, but then he would have had to sit by the big window eating his egg with Mrs. Grouch's furry bangs pressed against the plate glass, her bright eyes watching every bite he took, her little tongue dripping hungrily.

The rains lasted a long time that spring, keeping on until June. Mrs. Grouch stood the home her old man had provided for her as long as she could. The babies were growing and taking up more room, the roof leaked, and Old Grouch always took the dry side. When the wind blew from the north there might as well have been no roof at all. One afternoon while Jerome was tramping in the woods, snug in oilskins and rubber boots, she moved her babies into the house. Helping herself to the stuffing in his mattress, she made a nest in the oven. She had long ago learned how to open the oven door. The smell of the oven pleased her. It had a faint food smell which was elegant. She could feed her babies and lick the oven walls, nibbling bits of burned meat as she came to them.

Jerome discovered the family at once because the oven door was open. He did not scold about the mattress when she showed him her brood of silky raccoons. But he was hungry and this was Saturday afternoon. Jerome always fixed a beef roast for Saturday supper. Once a week the mailman left the meat in his mailbox at the foot of the hill. Jerome got a wooden box and put it in a corner, then he moved the family. Mrs. Grouch was miffed, but she accepted the change with a sly smile. Later she would slip her family back into the oven.

Old Grouch stamped up on the porch and seated himself in the open doorway. He scolded his wife in proper style; he glared at Jerome and tossed a few nasty cracks at him. Between growls he kept sniffing the roast cooking in the oven, and shaking his fur to get the raindrops off it. With a final warning to his wife he turned about, climbed the redwood trunk, and got into his nest. The wind was from the north, and his wife was not there to keep the rain off his back. He stayed in the nest for half an hour, then he climbed back down the tree trunk and walked to the door. Jerome grinned at him. He was cutting the roast. He sliced off a piece and laid it on a saucer. He set the saucer on the floor.

Old Grouch looked at the saucer. This was dangerous

business. Going into a cabin was like stepping into a box trap. But he was wet and cold; his wife had walked out on him. He needed food and warmth. Ruffling his scruff, he walked into the house. He paused at the saucer and sniffed the good smell of the roast. He took a bite. When Mrs. Grouch scurried across the floor to share with him, he caught up the piece of meat in his forepaws. He sat up and glowered at her. Then he began munching the roast. His wife sniffed eagerly. She looked up at Jerome. He handed her a slice of meat. She took it and seated herself beside her husband. They sat there eating very much like humans, using their small hands to tear bits of meat from the large pieces, then stuffing the bits into their mouths.

By the time Jerome had finished his supper Old Grouch had made up his mind. He had marched to the door three times, and each time the cold rain had spattered into his face. He knew his wife and babies were going to sleep warm and dry inside the cabin. She had already returned to the box, where she sat with her small black eyes just above the edge. Old Grouch felt he could do with some more roast, too. He was still a bit hungry. He would stay in the cabin.

After the dishes were washed Jerome lighted his pipe. He was faced with a new problem. He had been trying for weeks to get Old Grouch into the cabin. Now that the old fellow and his family had moved in he dared not close the door. If he closed the door it was hard to say what Old Grouch would do. Jerome was sure it would be pretty wild.

But the night air was growing chilly. The wind was blowing into the room, wet and cold. Even if he did chase Old Grouch out into the rain he couldn't put Mrs. Grouch and the babies out. Jerome got to his feet. Old Grouch took one look at Jerome towering above him, then scuttled out into the night.

Jerome set the gasoline mantel lamp on the table so the white light would flood the door. He got his tool chest from under the bed. Mrs. Grouch kept her eyes just above the edge of the box. Jerome cut a small door in the bottom of his big door. He swung the small door by a pair of butterfly hinges and bored three holes in it.

As he gathered up his saw and auger and screw driver Jerome realized that the little door would offer welcome to any and all who roamed. It would mean keeping open house to all, except, of course, those neighbors too big to squeeze through the little door. He had never been able to make friends; it might be that the little door would change everything. He took the lamp and examined the chimney of his fireplace. The little skunks were not sleeping on the damper, so he lighted the fire he had laid earlier in the day. Pulling his padded chair up to the fireplace, he set his tobacco jar on the chair arm. As an afterthought he got a saucer and stacked a few squares of roast on it. He set the saucer on the floor beside the chair.

Jerome puffed slowly on his pipe. He watched the red tongues of flame lick around the oak and madroña logs in the fireplace. The beating warmth made him feel drowsy. He was on his second pipe when Old Grouch solved the mystery of the little door. He had peeped in through the three holes and discovered that Jerome had turned out the gasoline lamp, that his wife was snug and dry in the box with the babies. He sniffed and caught the rich smell of roast beef. He was wet and cold. He eased through the little door just as his wife hopped from the box, carrying one of the babies. She had her teeth set in the scruff. Shaking the water from his fur, he watched her put the youngster into the oven. He scowled at her, but he didn't make a sound. The warmth of the fireplace and the smell of the roast in the saucer drew him. He moved warily toward the fire. His experience with men had made him wary. But he was cold and he had an idea he could eat some more. Seating himself in the deep shadows near the chair, he stretched his snout toward the dish. He kept his eyes on Jerome. When Jerome did not move Old Grouch eased forward and picked up a piece of meat. He sat up and began munching it.

Mrs. Grouch had finished transferring her babies to the oven. She sat on the door for a while, watching the two males at the fireplace. Shaking her head, she turned her back upon them and curled up with her brood.

Jerome had never been able to talk with people. He had always known he was missing a great deal, but he had never been able to say the weather was nice or that the weather was bad when people came into his shop. He set his pipe on the arm of the chair and tossed another log on the fire. Old Grouch ducked into a patch of deep shadow, but he came out again and got another piece of meat. The warmth of the fire was beating against his fur. He felt contented and happy. Jerome leaned back and spoke out loud. When he spoke the sound of his voice startled even himself. Old Grouch, now gorged with roast and sleepy from the heat, toppled off the hearth and had to make quite an effort to right himself. Mrs. Grouch thrust her head out of the oven and stared at Jerome wildly. If it had not been for her babies she would have fled into the night.

"When I came up here I was licked," Jerome had said. It was as though a stranger had spoken to him; he heard his own voice so seldom. He felt called upon to answer the stranger.

"And were you licked?"

Old Grouch batted his eyes fearfully. He looked all around the room but saw no human being except Jerome, whom he had ceased to consider a man, because Jerome never shouted or whistled or talked at all.

"I've spent a lifetime carving cherubs and angels on tombstones. I've cut many a nice sentiment on a gravestone, but never was able to recite a single line before company." Jerome pointed his pipestem toward the fire. "It's a sad business, dealing with sad people, and not being able to say a word to comfort them."

Old Grouch braced himself and let his stomach ease down until he was resting comfortably. He had room for a bite or two more, and the fire was very nice. Jerome smiled down at him. Old Grouch looked like a small bandit with the black patches which circled his eyes and extended along his cheeks like black bands, making a perfect mask against the lighter coloring of his fur. He cocked his head. He was in a mellow mood. His stomach was full to bursting; his furry hide was warm. He felt like singing.

He started out with a soft "Shur-r-r-r," then went into a deeper note, a long-drawn, tremulous "Whoo-oo-oo," not unlike the call of a screech owl, only softer and sweeter, much more mellow. Jerome's smile widened. He had never dared venture a note himself. In all of the hundreds of times he had sat alone in his pew in church he had never dared open his mouth and sing.

"I have missed much," he said.

"Whoo-oo-oo," Old Grouch sang, his head swaying sleepily.

From the oven door came an answering trill. Never had Mrs. Grouch heard her husband put so much tenderness, so much romance into his song. It touched her deeply, so deeply she closed her eyes and sang back to him. Jerome laid down his pipe.

Turning to catch the high soprano from the oven, Jerome noticed that the little door was bobbing back and forth. He fixed his attention upon it. A small head with black shoe-button eyes appeared. The head moved into the room, followed by a slim body. A moment later another slim body moved through the door. Two tall white plumes lifted. The little spotted skunks had come visiting. Papa waved his plume and stamped his feet; Mama waved her plume and stamped her feet. Like a good host, Jerome arose from his chair. Instantly the two little skunks vanished through the door. Jerome filled a saucer with canned milk and set it near the door, then he went back to his chair before the fire.

Almost at once the little door opened and the skunks marched in. They sat down and began lapping eagerly. When Mrs. Grouch hopped off the oven door and

started toward the saucer, Papa elevated his plume and stamped his forefeet. He rushed at her, did a handstand, flipped his hind feet down again, then stamped some more. Mrs. Grouch knew what that meant, as did every other living thing in the woods. She hastily retreated to the oven door. Papa went back to his milk.

Jerome leaned back in his chair. Old Grouch was in full voice now; his whoo-oo-oo was deep and bell-like. Jerome tried an experimental note himself. He was amazed at its quality. It was a baritone note with feeling and depth in it. But it sent Mrs. Grouch scrambling back into the oven; Papa and Mama left without waiting to stamp their feet. Only Old Grouch was not startled at all. He just sat and swayed back and forth and sang.

He seemed to have caught the fine flavor of Jerome's baritone. Jerome tried a few more notes. Mrs. Grouch stayed in the oven; the spotted skunks stayed under the floor. Old Grouch picked up the last square of roast and ate it slowly. When he swallowed it his stomach bulged bigger. He cocked an eye at Jerome. Jerome tried

a few hymns he remembered. Old Grouch joined in. He had only one song, but it blended well with any hymn.

After a bit Jerome began to feel sleepy. He was sleepy and he was happy. He leaned back and closed his eyes. Old Grouch yawned. He ambled toward the oven door. After two tries he managed to hop up on the door. Easing into the oven, he curled up with his family. Jerome sighed deeply. Here among friends he could talk about things he had always wanted to talk about, and he could sing when he felt like it. He got to his feet and took his flannel nightgown from its hook. He smiled as he got ready for bed.

CHAPTER TWO

JEROME KILDEE might have lived to a ripe old age in his house on the top of his mountain without ever knowing anything about his neighbors if he had not discovered that he could talk and sing too. Once a man finds he can talk, his neighbors are more likely to be friendly. Jerome did not go visiting, but he was pleasant and talked quite a bit when one of his neighbors dropped in on him one Saturday afternoon.

His visitor was one of the nine Eppys. Emma Lou Eppy had been wanting to visit Jerome's cabin for a long time. She had met him a number of times down at the mailbox. His silence when she spoke to him had made her afraid of him. Then, shortly after Jerome and Old Grouch had enjoyed their evening of song, she met him again. She would have scooted past him, but he smiled at her. Emma Lou smiled back.

"Good morning, Mr. Kildee," she said.

"It is a fine morning," Jerome agreed. "A fine morning, indeed." It seemed to Emma Lou that he was tasting the words the way you would taste a candy bar. And she was right; Jerome was finding it very nice to say it was a nice day.

After he had gone up the trail leading to his house Emma Lou decided she would pay him a visit. She had a very definite reason for wanting to make friends with Jerome. She was having a bitter feud with Donald Roger Cabot. If she had the run of Jerome's hill, that would extend her territory right into the Cabot back yard. When Emma Lou declared war on anyone she meant business. Where the Eppys came from, mountain folks carried on their feuds in a serious manner. The battle had started over Donald Roger's dog, Strong Heart, a Doberman pup of the bluest blood. With Donald Roger along to do the sicking, Strong Heart was a deadly enemy to cats and to all wild animals in the woods.

With her scheme in her head, Emma Lou took the mail to the Eppy house. Usually the Eppys got only mail addressed to "Rural Box Holder," but today there was a letter from a fur house in St. Louis for Ben Eppy, the youngest son.

The Eppy house stood in a redwood grove which is known to the romantic-minded as a temple. The mother tree had surrounded herself with a circle of children.

CHAPTER TWO

The children were now grown to giant size, and the mother tree had long since vanished. The giants stood in a stately circle around a shady patio like padres guarding a shrine. The green twilight and the silence of a redwood temple never fail to draw the passer-by into its shade, and many a wanderer has built a house inside a grove only to feel the cold displeasure of the padres. A damp clamminess creeps into the beds in the house, the wallpaper turns green, and the chill gets into the bones of the dwellers. The smoke is pushed back down the chimney. Someone had built a house in this temple and later had abandoned it after braving the displeasure of the big trees for a season or two.

One spring the Eppys came chugging along the side road in their old truck. There were just six Eppys at that time. Job Eppy halted the truck in the shade of the biggest tree. He slid his long legs from under the steering wheel and eased himself out of the old truck. Cilly got out. The boys piled off the stack of household stuff in the back. Muck, Reddy, and Ma Grady, the Eppy hounds, hustled sniffs around the base of the big tree, awed at seeing a tree so big that proper sniffing called for quite a run.

"Mighty pretty place," Cilly said.

Job just looked up at the great trees. He came from a timber country, but he had never seen such trees before. Amby, the oldest boy, started toward the cabin, eager to search for treasure. Amby, being fourteen, had explored many deserted cabins and knew that someone was always ahead of you. But that did not dampen his eagerness. There might be something overlooked. Different folks looked for different things. His three brothers ran after him. Amby saw as soon as he stepped into the big main room that many people had explored this house. Most of its windowpanes were broken; old magazines littered the floor; a pile of rusting tin cans and brown bottles lay in a corner. Amby kicked a can across the floor.

"Shucks," he said.

"Smells ratty," Enoch said.

Cilly and Job stepped to the door. When Cilly looked into the house she said breathlessly:

"Job, it's got a wooden floor in it."

The Eppys moved right in, and after a while Job located the owner and bought the house and the bottom land below it. The Eppys liked the wilderness, the timber land, and the steep slopes choked with brush. Job cut timber for fences and for wood, but he would as soon have cut off a leg as to cut down one of the redwoods. Oak and madroña fell before the Eppy axes, and the wood was sold in town. Like many another family coming to California, the Eppys added a bit of their own way of life to their new home. The grove was soon littered with old cars and trucks and odds and ends Job picked up in trades.

Emma Lou loved the place. This was home. She loved the redwood walls of the house which had turned deep brown with age; she thought the fireplace Job and Amby had built was a masterpiece. By the time the Eppy family had reached nine members Job had added three rooms to the house.

Before Jerome had bought the hundred-acre hill the Eppys had considered it a part of their domain and had hunted and trapped over it. But as soon as Jerome moved in they kept their hounds at home and seldom hunted on his land. Job believed a good neighbor minded his own business and did not trespass unless invited to hunt. Jerome had never made any attempt to get friendly, so the Eppys stayed off his land.

Emma Lou dropped Ben's letter on the kitchen table. Cilly was shelling peas at the sink. "Fur list for Ben," Emma Lou said as she moved out of the kitchen fast. Cilly might think of something she ought to be doing if she stayed around. She was out of hearing before Cilly thought of anything.

Emma Lou knew a trail which wound up the hill through brush and heavy timber. Job and his sons had not trespassed upon Jerome's land, but Emma Lou had been over every foot of it. She did not hunt or trap, but she liked to hike and climb trees and watch Jerome's friends as they went about their business. She knew more about the animals on Jerome's hill than he did.

She was delayed in arriving at Jerome's house because she detoured past a fern-choked dell where a black-tailed doe had cached her fawn. Emma Lou crawled through a blackberry patch with some damage to her arms and bare legs. The doe was away feeding. When Emma Lou parted the ferns over the baby's bed the fawn played dead. Emma Lou tickled its ear. The fawn flapped its ear, then plastered it against its neck very quickly. Emma Lou let the ferns swing back into place. When she got back to the trail she looked as though she had been in a cat fight. Standing there, she frowned. She was thinking about Donald Roger Cabot.

"Just let me catch that dog chasing my deer," she said, and balled her fingers into fists. "Just let me catch him out in the woods." Her hand dropped to her hip pocket, where the handle of a beany stuck out a couple of inches. She had a dozen marbles in a side pocket. Marbles did not curve like stones when they were shot; they went straight as a bullet. With six brothers as teachers Emma Lou had learned much about the art of using a beany.

She moved on up the trail, her anger mounting as she remembered the clash she had had with Donald Roger earlier that week. She had come upon them in the woods near the mailbox. Strong Heart was worrying a possum he had flushed, and Donald Roger was urging him on. Emma Lou's beany had settled Strong Heart's hash, but it had cost her a prized marble. In her haste to save the possum she had shot the dog with her bird's-eye glassy. A hasty retreat had saved Donald Roger from suffering the same fate as his dog. Strong Heart had arrived home with a knot on his rump as big as a hen's egg.

Emma Lou always went over exciting events when she was alone in the woods. Sometimes she acted out things she hoped would happen; sometimes she just went back over things that had happened and thought of how she could have said or done something else. She had thought of a lot of things she could have done to Donald Roger, things she would do the next time she met him out in the woods sending his dog after a poor possum. She was flushed and angry when she burst from the woods above Jerome's cabin. Slowing down, she fanned her face with her straw hat.

As she looked at the house her curiosity made her forget she was angry. She had looked at the house from the cover of the woods, but she had never seen the inside of it. Mr. Kildee certainly had a very fine window; she had never seen such a window, outside of a store in town. She began to worry. He might be grouchy and look at her the way he usually did. Then she remembered he had smiled at her down at the mailbox, and he had said it was a very nice day. She stepped to the door and found it open.

When she looked into the room she saw Jerome seated at his table. Old Grouch and his wife sat on the floor with their children near them. They were seated in a small circle and they were all eating busily. Emma Lou blinked. She thought she must be seeing things, but no, she wasn't. A soft thud made her look toward Jerome's fireplace. She saw two little spotted skunks hop down out of the chimney. They shook soot from their fur before seating themselves upon the hearth. Sitting there, they eyed Jerome and grinned.

"Hello," Emma Lou said.

Jerome turned his head. When he saw Emma Lou he smiled. When he spoke his voice was very friendly. "Won't you come in? We're eating. You can join us."

Old Grouch stared hard at Emma Lou. His wife smiled sweetly, but she began shooing her babies toward the box in the corner. Jerome cast an eye toward the little skunks. There might be trouble if they decided to dash out through the door and got this girl excited. But the little skunks did not dash anyplace. They were busy washing soot off their white spots. They were traveled folks; they knew all about the nine Eppys and their

house, especially the cellar, which housed quite a few families of mice. They knew Emma Lou better than they knew Jerome. They had lived for a time in her cellar. The Eppy hounds had caused them to seek other quarters.

Emma Lou entered the cabin. She sat down on the floor. Papa and Mama walked up to her. They sat up and regarded her intently, their eyes watching her hands and then moving to the little pocket in her blouse. Emma Lou looked up at Jerome.

"I came off without any scraps," she said.

Jerome handed her a strip of crisp bacon. Emma Lou broke it into bits. She gave a small piece to each little skunk. They broke into loud churring sounds as they ate the bacon. Emma Lou laughed.

"Nice little stinkers, aren't they?" She looked up at Jerome.

Old Grouch snarled, then he dashed for the door. He was so fat he really wobbled. He reminded Emma Lou of a duck. When he got outside he began calling names in a very loud voice.

"He's Old Grouch," Jerome said. "But once you get to know him, he isn't bad company."

"He licked Ma Grady to a frazzle," Emma Lou said. "I guess he can smell hound on me. Of course Ma Grady is getting awfully old." She looked out at Old Grouch, who was seated on the doorstone. "Don't think he could do it now, he's too fat."

"Who's Ma Grady?" Jerome asked.

"One of our hound-dogs." Emma Lou reached out and gathered Mama into her arms. Jerome held his breath. Mama churred happily as she nosed for bits of bacon inside Emma Lou's hand. Papa climbed up and joined her. When the bacon was all gone she set them on the floor and they marched outside. They put the run on Old Grouch and took over the doorstone.

Emma Lou got to her feet. She gave her attention to the inside of the cabin. She had been looking at everything while she fed the skunks, but she hadn't wanted to seem impolite or curious. She admired the fireplace and the bark wall before she got to the part that really had her curious, the buttons dangling from the ceiling.

"What are they for?" she asked.

Jerome got to his feet. He was eager to demonstrate his inventions. He pulled a button and a cupboard door opened. He pulled another button and a drawer popped out.

"I figured them out to fool Mrs. Grouch," he explained.

Mrs. Grouch had hopped out of her box the instant the drawer popped open. It was the egg drawer, and she thought Jerome was going to have an egg. She looked disappointed when he shoved the drawer shut without taking out an egg.

"You have the most wonderful house I've ever seen," Emma Lou said. "And you have nice friends. But when Donald Roger Cabot and his town hound get up here there'll be trouble." She shook her red head and scowled. "But he won't trouble you any. I'll take care of that."

Jerome didn't know just what to say. He had met Donald Roger and Strong Heart a number of times, and he had been a bit worried. But he had never seen them very high on the side of his mountain. He smiled suddenly.

"Strong Heart? The name hardly fits his dog."

"I'll say not," Emma Lou said. "That hound is afraid of his own shadow. Cabot sicks him on, but he won't tackle anything unless it runs away from him."

Jerome grinned. She looked really angry. He shoved another chair up to the table. "I'll set a plate on for you," he said.

Emma Lou sat down. Her anger vanished as quickly as it had flared up. She laughed when Mrs. Grouch came trotting over to the table. Leaning down, she scratched her behind the ears.

"I don't have any milk except canned," Jerome said as he set the coffeepot on the table.

"I'll have coffee, black," she said.

"I drink it sort of strong," Jerome said uncertainly.

"Me too. I'm no sissy pants. Someday I'll be six feet tall like my brothers, and just as tough."

Jerome saw she wasn't joking. He poured a cup of coffee for her and shoved the sugar across the table. Emma Lou ignored the sugar. She took bacon and jam and bread. As Jerome watched her drink the black coffee he wondered why her folks let her have it. But she had a fine appetite; she ate twice as much as he ever ate at one meal. As she ate she kept looking at his fireplace.

"You have a wonderful fireplace," she said.

"Made it myself." There was a touch of pride in Jerome's voice.

"You could make lots of money building fireplaces," Emma Lou said.

Jerome shook his head. "I'm not doing any more stonework. I walled my tools in back of the last stone. I guess I'll let them stay there."

"What do you do?" Emma Lou asked.

"Nothing," Jerome said, and smiled.

"That must be swell." She sighed. "This is my idea of how to live."

They chatted on for a while. Old Grouch came in after the skunks went away. He waddled over to the box and carried on an argument with his wife in an undertone. Emma Lou helped with the dishes. When they were stacked away she knew she must go. The Eppys went in for heavy suppers. Her mother would be getting things ready. In about an hour Cilly would need her. That hour would give her time to circle around by the Cabot place, just to look things over.

"I'll have to run along," she said. "But I've had a good time."

"Come back again," Jerome said as he stepped to the door with her.

"I will, and very soon," Emma Lou promised.

CHAPTER THREE

AN EVENT of considerable importance happened very shortly after Emma Lou visited Jerome. The spotted skunk family increased in number. Jerome and Papa were very much excited about it. Papa dashed about wildly, ducking up the chimney, under the bed, and then out of the house. He never went under the floor. Jerome got the idea he was banned from the nest for the time being. Jerome wrenched his shoulder trying to get his head under the foundation far enough to see the new family. But the skunks were black in color, so he could not see them in the dim light under the house. For once Jerome was sorry he was such a good stone-worker. He had built the foundation strong and tight. There was only the small opening he had left for ventilation.

Jerome considered removing a board from the floor. The trouble was, he did not know which board to take up. He crawled over the floor, putting his ear to every other board. Papa dashed about, jumping upon chairs, dancing a wild jig for a minute, then listening with Jerome. The way Papa was acting was what made Jerome worry. He was sure Mama was in dire need of help. He was certain Papa was trying to make him understand he ought to do something. It was not until he came to the third board out from the fireplace that he knew everything was all right. He could hear Mama churring happily and small voices squeaking. Jerome sat up and grinned at Papa. He got out his pipe and filled it. When it was going good he spoke to Papa, who was fidgeting on the edge of the fireplace.

"Well," he said. "Everything is just fine down there."

Papa showed his teeth. He wrinkled his nose as a wisp of tobacco smoke floated around his head. Giving Jerome a disgusted look, he marched out of the cabin. Jerome was not sure why Papa was disgusted. Jerome guessed that there was a law laid down by Dame Nature which barred Papa from the nest at a time like this. He got to his feet and walked to the door. When he saw Papa stalking off toward the woods he was sure he had guessed right. Papa wasn't welcome in the nest for a while.

Later Mama showed up. She was very proud and happy, and very hungry. Papa had returned from the woods. Jerome guessed he had been ordered to stay under the floor to keep the babies warm while Mama got something to eat. He gave Mama a saucer of milk and a thick slice of Spam.

Mrs. Grouch was very much interested in Mama's family, but she didn't go poking about near the ventilator hole. Old Grouch sat in the sun and leered at Papa when he finally showed up. He seemed to be showing off. He had never cared for the babies while Mrs. Grouch got something to eat. It was clear he didn't think much of the way Papa was letting Mama push him around. Every once in a while he would burp lazily as he sat with his paws folded over his fat stomach, then he would put on his sneer again.

The arrival of the little skunks, who would soon be demanding meat, should have sent the mice and the pack rats on their way, but they did not go. The mother pack rat had gone to a lot of trouble gnawing a hole under the eave so that she could get down between the siding and the wallboard at a spot near the fireplace where the wall stayed warm. She had no intention of leaving a heated apartment. With any luck at all she would soon have one whole section between the studding filled with things she had pilfered. Her collection included a pair of Jerome's pliers, three spools of thread, two white and one black, his eye cup, a quarter and four dimes, which Jerome had carelessly left on his stand. These were stored along with an assortment of pine cones, pine needles, cactus thorns, pretty rocks, and plain grass. There was a liberal supply of thorny bushes and spiny branches. How she managed to sleep com-

fortably on such a bed was a secret known only to a pack rat. She had three babies in the nest, and she had driven her mate away as soon as the babies came. Papa had left her alone because it was easier to catch mice than to get at her. He was waiting for the young rats to get big enough to venture out into the open. But now that a heavy burden had been placed upon him he began sniffing around and planning ways of raiding her nest. He spent hours under the oven near the hole she had gnawed. He always pretended to be asleep. Jerome had a feeling it would only be a matter of time before Papa and Mama dined upon young rat.

In a way Jerome was sorry, but he knew very well that if Papa didn't clean out the rat family he'd have to do it himself. As the young rats got bigger they joined their mother in thumping their feet on the wall. They were always most active from midnight until dawn, and they liked a section of the wall only a few feet from the head of Jerome's bed. Why a soft-footed rat should clump loudly like a man on stilts, Jerome could not guess, but clump they did, and very loudly. His faith in Papa was strong, and after a few nights he knew Papa was coming through. He kept track of the casualties among the rats by the lessening of the thumping sounds. Within a week after the arrival of Papa's children the thumping had diminished to a solitary round of rappings. Jerome thought it sounded sad and lonesome. He was glad the sounds did not stop entirely. If the mother rat eluded Papa there would be another family.

Jerome was beginning to think Emma Lou had forgotten her promise to visit him again. He was sorry because he liked Emma Lou. She had given him a new slant on girls. Jerome had always thought of girls as sweet little things dressed in fluffy gowns with scrubbed, pink faces, and neat pigtails down their backs. Emma Lou did not fit this picture at all. Her hair was bright red, and it was bobbed. She wore jeans rolled up to her knees, and her face usually had smudges or berry-vine scratches on it. She had quite a few freckles too. Now that Jerome was making it his job to study the folks around him, he was very much interested in Emma Lou. He decided he liked her better than he would have liked one of the girls he had always had in his mind. She had a big smile and a tiptilted nose that was very nice.

Then Emma Lou showed up. The long rubber bands and the leather pouch of her beany dangled from her hip pocket. She was carrying her hat in her hands. It was heaping full of blackberries. They weren't little wild berries; they were big ones off the bush at home. She set the hat on the table.

"Hello," she called to Jerome, who was laying a fire in the fireplace.

"Hello. Fine morning." Jerome dumped a log into the fireplace and turned around.

"Everything under control?" she asked. "That Donald Cabot been bothering you any?"

When Jerome shook his head she went over to the box in the corner and lifted one of the Grouch children from its nest. Mrs. Grouch hopped out of the box and sat up, eying Emma Lou anxiously.

"Haven't seen a sign of Donald or his dog," Jerome said.

Emma Lou grinned. There was a wicked flicker in her green eyes as she nodded her head. "Didn't think you would," she said, and let it go at that.

Jerome finished laying the fire. He was glad Emma Lou had come. He felt like talking, and there was news. "What have you been doing?" he asked, just to be polite. He would save the news about Papa and Mama until just the right moment.

"I went over to Santa Cruz and visited my aunt," Emma Lou said. She frowned darkly. "Had a rotten time. Aunt Tilly's always scandalized by jeans. Cilly made me wear skirts all the time I was there."

Jerome nodded. By this time he knew who Cilly was. He clucked his tongue in sympathy. "Must have been pretty bad," he said.

"It sure was." Emma Lou had seated herself on the floor. She had the raccoon family in her lap. They were busily trying to pull the buttons off her shirt. She shook her head, then she grinned at Jerome. "It wasn't all of it so bad. Uncle Will and I overhauled his pickup truck. I did the underneath stuff because Uncle Will has too much stomach."

Mrs. Grouch, seeing that she had a baby sitter, walked out into the sunshine. She headed down the slope at a fast trot. This was the first time she had had a chance to roam in the woods without her brood tagging her. Old Grouch roused himself enough to sit up, but he did not follow her. He yawned and lay down again.

"She shouldn't be prowling in the woods in the daytime," Emma Lou said. "You're spoiling your raccoons. They should prowl after dark."

"I don't try to make them do anything," Jerome said. "They don't belong to me."

Emma Lou considered this for a long minute. It was a new idea. When her brothers tamed anything it was their property. She had thought of the raccoons and the skunks as something Jerome owned.

"That's the way it ought to be," she said at last. "I'll keep an eye on her little ones until she comes back. These little nuts would wander off and get lost."

"I don't think they'd get lost," Jerome said. "They're about big enough to take care of themselves. She's been taking them for long walks in the woods lately."

"Where're the spotted skunks?" Emma Lou asked suddenly. "In the chimney?"

Jerome grinned eagerly. "They have a family under the floor." He was tickled when she showed excitement over the news.

"How many?" she asked.

"Don't know. I tried to get a peek at them, but it's too dark under the floor. Sounds like quite a family." He chuckled. "Keeps the old man humping to catch enough mice for Mama these days, and she sees to it that he does the hunting. Been good for my sleep, though."

"Why?" she asked.

"Pack rat family's been thumping inside the wall near my bed. It got so I couldn't get any sleep. But after Papa had to start really hunting, the noise slacked off."

"Good thing," Emma Lou said. "Rats smell a place up." She put the little raccoon on the floor. "I'll keep an eye on them, but I just have to have a peek at the little skunks." She stood up and dusted her hands off. "How old are they?"

"Over a week," Jerome said. He doubted she'd be able to get a peek at the skunk family.

She nodded toward the berries. "I picked a few for your dinner."

"I'll make shortcake," Jerome said. "Have a peek at the family if you can."

Emma Lou turned toward the door. She paused to poke a finger into the ball of fur in the square of sun near the window. The ball of fur exploded into a raccoon. Old Grouch growled at her and arched his back. His neck fur swelled out around his face and he looked very fierce. Emma Lou laughed, and Old Grouch bared his teeth. Then he turned his back on her and curled up again. This time he left one eye open. If she tried to poke him again he'd grab her finger. She didn't try again; she walked out into the sunshine.

Jerome busied himself making shortcake batter. Cooking was the only job he had really applied himself to since coming to the mountain. He was rather proud of his cooking. By the time the shortcake was in the oven and the berries sugared and mashed, he began to wonder what had happened to Emma Lou. Stepping to the door, he looked out.

At first he saw only her legs and hiking boots waving in the air beside the wall. Moving out on the doorstone, he saw she was lying on the ground. Before her sat Papa and Mama. They were beaming proudly. Close to Emma Lou's face squirmed five little skunks. They looked like mice and they wiggled helplessly. Before Jerome could move Mama picked up one of the babies and ducked under the floor. Papa stood guard, and a minute later Mama came back after another baby. Jerome did not move until all of the babies had been carried back to the nest.

"You got her to bring them out," he said admiringly.

Emma Lou rolled over. She locked her fingers back

of her head and looked up at Jerome dreamily. "They're so wonderfully soft and silky, and so helpless," she said.

"Look like mice," Jerome said. "Mice without much hair."

"They do not," Emma Lou said. "Two of them look like Papa, three look like Mama. I'm going to name them."

Jerome grinned. "Be nice. But you better wait till you can tell them apart."

"I can now—that is, almost," Emma Lou said. She sat up. "Wonder if anyone ever had a skunk and raccoon circus? I've heard of flea circuses. If you can train a flea it should be easy to teach skunks and raccoons to do tricks."

Jerome considered the idea. It had a number of interesting angles. "You might try it," he said. "You sure have a way with animals."

"I'll bet it would be easy," Emma Lou said. "I'll have to make some things like they have in a circus—tubs and stands and some little rings for them to do stunts on."

Jerome suddenly remembered the shortcake and rushed inside to have a peek at it. It was browning nicely. He shoved a stick of wood into the stove and got out dishes. Emma Lou came in and sat down beside the table. Her head was buzzing with the circus idea.

"Old Grouch will be the ringmaster," she said softly. "He looks just like one."

Jerome grinned at her. "With seven spotted skunks to handle, he'll be mighty busy."

"They'll have to learn manners." Emma Lou sniffed eagerly. Jerome had taken the cake tins out of the oven. The two cakes were beauties and smelled good. When Jerome set the cakes on the table Emma Lou sighed. "I'm a terrible cook," she said. "If I'd made those cakes they wouldn't be any thicker than pancakes. Cilly won't ever let me try a cake any more. She says I'm hopeless." Then she grinned. "But it's O.K. If I could bake cakes like these I'd have to stay home and cook."

Jerome poured the sweetened berries over the first layer, then stacked the second layer on and poured on more berries. He poised a long knife over the cake.

"We'll cut it in two. Any left on our plates will go to the raccoons."

"They'll beg their share before we finish," Emma Lou said. She was looking at the row of baby raccoons seated near her chair. They had their eyes fixed upon the cake and were licking their lips.

Jerome waved the knife back and forth, then let it settle down. It was halfway through the first layer when they heard the loud barking of a dog. Emma Lou leaped out of her chair. As she charged through the door she jerked her beany from her pocket. Jerome raised the knife. He stared after her. Then he heard a cry he recognized. It was the wailing cry of Mrs. Grouch, and Jerome knew she was in trouble. Old Grouch came to life with surprising speed. He was out through the door before Jerome could move. Jerome hurried outside, and once he was out in the yard, he started running. Emma Lou had just vanished into the woods below the house. Old Grouch was making good time, but Jerome passed him, spurred on by the wild cries from Mrs. Grouch.

Jerome burst out of a thicket into a small clearing. He was gasping for breath and slowed to a walk when he saw Emma Lou. She was facing Donald Roger Cabot, and her voice rang out furiously.

"You murderer!"

Then Jerome saw Strong Heart. He was worrying something in the grass back of Donald Roger. Donald Roger was facing Emma Lou. He had his chin thrust out aggressively. Emma Lou jumped to one side. She raised her beany and pulled the rubber bands back to her ear. The next instant Strong Heart shot into the air with a howl of anguish. He staggered around in a circle, then charged away into the timber.

Jerome ran forward. Emma Lou was digging another marble out of her pocket. Donald Roger had backed away, but he was not running; he was facing Emma Lou.

She stretched the rubber bands again and the beany snapped. An oak branch not more than six inches from Donald Roger's ear exploded and shot into the air.

"You shot my dog!" he shouted.

"I did, and I'm going to pot you between the eyes!" Emma Lou yelled.

Jerome caught her arm. "Now, now. You can't do that." His voice sounded strange and tight.

Emma Lou's arm dropped suddenly. She pulled away from Jerome and ran to where Mrs. Grouch lay in the grass. She gathered the limp raccoon in her arms and rocked back and forth. Then she started crying. The tears splashed down upon the bundle of gray fur in her arms. Donald Roger had been staring at her haughtily. Now he looked uncomfortable. Jerome began to feel anger swelling up inside him. He should tell this boy to get off his land. But he couldn't say a word. He just looked at Donald Roger, and the boy began to squirm.

Emma Lou stopped rocking. She sniffed back the tears, then she looked at Donald Roger and her eyes began to blaze again. "Next time it won't be a beany. From now on I'm packin' Ben's rifle."

Donald Roger shifted from one foot to the other. He wanted to get away, but he wasn't running from any girl, not this Eppy girl. If she had been a boy he'd have waded into her. Strong Heart might be badly hurt, and she had come near hitting him.

"You better be careful," he muttered.

"I'm putting a bullet into that dog, and I'll dust you, too, if I catch you up here on this mountain." Emma Lou got to her feet and looked at Jerome. Tears were starting again. "She's dead," she said.

"How'd I know it was your pet raccoon?" Donald Roger asked.

Emma Lou thrust the body of Mrs. Grouch at Jerome. He caught the dead raccoon, and that kept him from catching Emma Lou. Donald Roger saw that it was time to swallow his pride and run for it. Emma Lou's hand went into her pocket and came out with a large glass marble. Donald Roger had only three jumps to make before he was under cover, and he made them fast. Emma Lou's beany whanged. Donald Roger crashed through a toyon bush.

"Just winged him," Emma Lou said bitterly.

Jerome's voice came back to him. "Serves him right and good," he said. Then he remembered what Emma Lou had said about carrying Ben's rifle and thought he had better smooth things over a little. "But you mustn't use a rifle on them," he said gently. "Just get you into trouble."

"Why not? He's a killer, isn't he?" Emma Lou asked savagely. Jerome didn't fully realize it, but he was looking at the daughter of a clan that had settled a good many fights with rifles. Emma Lou was all hillwoman as she stood there before him, and she wasn't California hillwoman either. It made Jerome feel uncomfortable.

"I'll bury her," he said. "Up back of the cabin."

"Just you leave that bird to me," she said. Then she added, "Yes, we'll have to bury her."

At that moment Old Grouch came puffing out of a thicket. He had been down the slope following Strong Heart's tracks. He had given up the chase after he found that the Doberman could run ten times as fast as he could. He waddled up to Jerome and looked up at the furry form in his arms. His scruff bristled, and he snarled savagely. Jerome had never seen Old Grouch so stirred up. After a minute the old raccoon turned about and ran off toward the house. He seemed to have remembered that his children had been left alone.

CHAPTER FOUR

JEROME AND EMMA LOU buried Mrs. Grouch under a madroña tree back of the house. Jerome patted the earth into a smooth mound, then he leaned on his shovel and looked down at the new grave. Emma Lou was on her hands and knees. She was holding Old Grouch back. He objected to having earth piled over the slim one, and he was growling and ruffing his fur and snapping at Emma Lou. But he did not bite her. He let her put an arm around him and pull him away. She looked up at Jerome.

"There should be a stone for a marker or something," she said.

Jerome thought of the tools sealed into his fireplace. He didn't say anything for quite a while. Finally he said, "I'll make a headstone for her." He moved the shovel a little and added, "I'll make a fine headstone for Mrs. Grouch."

Emma Lou blinked back tears. She smiled up at him. "That will be swell." She jumped to her feet, lifting Old Grouch up in her arms. He did not try to get away; his head pushed against her and he nestled down. "And from now on we'll have to take care of her babies."

The four youngsters were seated in a row on the doorstone. They were watching Jerome and Emma Lou. As they neared the cabin Old Grouch started growling at the children. They heard his growls and ducked for their box in the corner.

Papa and Mama were seated in the center of the table. They had sampled the shortcake. Their teeth marks showed all around the edge of the upper layer. The shortcake did not matter now. Emma Lou put Old Grouch down. She picked up Papa and Mama and set them on the floor. For once they did not scare Old Grouch. They walked out through the door quietly, their plumes elevated.

Jerome stood looking at the shortcake. It was soggy and slumped down on the plate. He set it on the floor, and the little raccoons gathered around it. Old Grouch sat by the stove, watching them, but he didn't go near the cake. It was the first time Jerome had ever seen him refuse food. Emma Lou said after a long silence:

"Ben says animals know. He says they can smell death."

Jerome nodded. Of course Old Grouch knew that tragedy had struck. He knew the slender one would not come back to her nest.

"Why are boys so hateful?" Emma Lou asked.

Jerome considered the question carefully. He had never given boys much thought. But now he remembered how he used to hunt squirrels and rabbits. He remembered one time when he had sicked his dog on the neighbor's cat. He shook his head and looked uncomfortable.

"Guess they aren't all that way," he said, but he didn't make it sound very convincing.

"They are, but Donald Roger Cabot is the worst. He's stuck-up and mean." Emma Lou's chin was up and her eyes were snapping.

Jerome remembered the threat she had made. He began to worry. "Best forget about it," he said. "I guess the boy didn't quite realize what he was doing. He thought he was chasing a wild raccoon."

"That dog of his needs shooting," Emma Lou said.

Jerome had to hide a smile. The smile started suddenly as he remembered the startled look that had come over the face of the Doberman when Emma Lou's marble hit him on the rump. The dog looked like a friendly sort. It was the boy's fault, of course. But he could not feel much sympathy for Strong Heart. The name made him want to smile too. It didn't seem to fit him very well. Jerome knew his anger was being tempered by worry over what Emma Lou would do to the Doberman and to Donald Roger. He was sure their next meeting would bring real trouble. He had to get her mind off them until she cooled off a bit.

"What shall we put on the headstone?" he asked.

"Can you carve a raccoon for the top?" she asked.

Jerome thought of the hundreds of lambs he had carved, of the angels and the cherubs. He nodded. "I can do a nice one," he said.

"We'll have to figure out what to say on the stone."

Emma Lou puckered her brows. "We can't say 'Mrs. Grouch.' We can't call her that. She was sweet and gentle."

"No," Jerome agreed. "I usually put on 'REST IN PEACE.' "

"That can go at the bottom." Emma Lou's face brightened. "I need a pencil and some paper."

Jerome got to his feet. He pulled a button, and a drawer popped open. "Have to keep the pencils in with the knives and forks to keep the pack rat from getting them," he explained. He took out a pencil, then got a sheet of paper from his stand.

Emma Lou sat looking at the paper for a long time. At last she looked up at Jerome. "I think Charmine is a beautiful name," she said. She had just read a book about a girl called Charmine who had been very beautiful, though a bit unlucky.

"Nice name," Jerome agreed.

Emma Lou wrote, "Charmine." Then she chewed the rubber on the pencil for a while. "How about putting 'A LOVELY LADY' under that?"

Jerome nodded. "And the date. We can't put the date of birth, but we can put 'PASSED AWAY JULY 27, 1948.' "

"And under that, 'REST IN PEACE.' " Emma Lou's pencil moved busily. When she had finished writing she nodded her head. "It will be very beautiful," she said softly.

And so Mrs. Grouch became Charmine, a lovely lady. She was freed from the influence of her grouchy husband and elevated to a high place in the memory of two who would remember her longer than anyone else.

Jerome got a chisel and a hammer. He removed the largest stone from the face of the fireplace. His tools were neatly stacked in the deep cavern he had made for them. The sight of them gave Jerome a feeling of eagerness. He realized that he had missed them. He took them out and laid them in a row on the table.

He had a few slabs of Monterey stone left over from building the fireplace. The cream-colored stone would work very well. Selecting a piece, he set it on the table and looked at it. Emma Lou hovered about hopefully.

"I'll have to think on it a bit," Jerome said. "Next time you come I'll have the raccoon cut in the top."

Emma Lou nodded. She understood that Jerome couldn't carve out a raccoon with her standing there looking at him. She couldn't write a letter with Ben looking over her shoulder, reading each word she wrote. "You'll keep an eye on her little ones?" she asked anxiously.

Jerome nodded. There wouldn't be much care needed. They had been eating meat for a long time. Their mother had had them out in the woods almost every day. He was sure they would start to prowl very soon, and he did not wish to keep them from their natural way of life.

"They're beginning to want to look around a bit," he said.

"You won't fasten the little door?"

"No," Jerome said. "Would you?"

Emma Lou hesitated. "No," she agreed. "But if they run away it will be lonesome."

Jerome considered this. He had thought about the raccoons quite a bit. He was sure they would go away into the woods and take up the life they were supposed to live. He had made up his mind not to try to make domestic animals out of them. They should do the things raccoons did. They couldn't just stay in the box until they grew as big as Old Grouch. For one thing, there wouldn't be room in the box.

"I guess they'll go off and be raccoons," he said.

"I hope they come back once in a while," Emma Lou said. "Of course I'm bound to meet them in the woods, but it would be nice if they made this their headquarters."

Jerome looked down at Old Grouch, who had seated

himself where he could look out through the window. He wondered if the old fellow would go out and find himself another mate. He smiled at Emma Lou.

"I think he'll stay with me."

"Yes, he'll stay," Emma Lou agreed. "Well, I better be running along. But I'll keep a closer watch on this hill from now on." There was a cold gleam in her eyes.

"I don't think you'll need a rifle," Jerome ventured.

"I'll pack one anyway," Emma Lou said. She got to her feet and walked to the door. "I'll see you tomorrow," she called over her shoulder.

Jerome watched her swing along across the clearing. He sighed deeply. He was going to miss Charmine, the lovely lady. The cabin would not be the same without her. He sat down and stared at the slab of Monterey stone. A feeling of eagerness began to grow inside him. He'd cut a head and forepaws, make her appear to be behind the stone and peeping over it, the way she always looked at him over the edge of the box. He took the stone out on the doorstone, then brought his tools out and laid them in a row. Very soon he was tapping away.

Jerome smiled as he shaped the stone. The rough form of a raccoon head began to appear at the top of the slab. The sun dipped toward distant San Francisco Bay. On the other side of the slope blue shadows stole in upon Monterey Bay. On the heels of the shadows came fog banks. Jerome chipped and shaped and smiled. When dusk forced him to stop working he carried the slab into the house and set it on the table.

When he lighted the gasoline lantern he discovered that Old Grouch had routed the children out of the box and was curled up in their nest. The children were huddled into a small heap under the stove. Jerome listened for a few minutes to the snores coming from the box, then he moved the slab of stone to the mantel over the fireplace and set about getting supper. He was hungry, having eaten nothing since breakfast, so he fried four eggs and four strips of bacon. Before the stove top was hot the young raccoons were awake and seated in a circle, watching eagerly. But no little lady had hopped out of the box in the corner when he pulled the button to release the egg drawer. Old Grouch did not stir.

Jerome boiled two of the eggs for the raccoons. He fried the other two with the bacon for himself. He made his coffee a bit stronger that night. When he sat down the four raccoons moved in to gather around the saucer, where he had set out crumbled egg and bits of bacon. The youngsters grumbled and chattered as they ate. They did not seem worried at all.

The meal was over before Old Grouch roused himself and climbed out of the box. Jerome boiled an egg for the old fellow. Old Grouch ate it, but without his usual zest. When he had finished he ambled back to the box and climbed into it. Curling up, he hid his nose in his furry brush and went to sleep. The children played about for a while. Jerome watched them as they romped.

The largest of them was a fine fellow with extra-large patches around his eyes. For some time he had been challenging his mother's authority and paying little heed to her advice. The smallest raccoon was a trim little miss hardly half as big as the sleek one. She had been a trial to her mother and had been punished more than any of the others. She was always teasing the others and getting nipped for it, then wailing loudly. Her mother had worked out a plan for punishing her. She would leave the runt in the box when she took her family down to the spring for a romp just before dark. Jerome wondered what trouble her new freedom would get her into.

Suddenly the sleek one started toward the little door. The others marched after him, with Runt bringing up the rear. They marched out through the little door one at a time. Runt paused to peep around the little door before she ran after the others. Jerome had an idea they were going out to look for their mother.

He washed the few dishes he had used. When the table was cleared he set the stone slab on it so the light struck it just right. Sitting back, he looked at his work. He had a feeling this would be his finest piece of work; certainly it was the first piece thought out and created all by himself. Back in his shop he had always made things people wanted, things other stonecutters had made before him. True, he had always given the faces of the angels and of the cherubs an expression he liked. But he had been carving designs his grandfather and then his father had carved. He was impatient to finish the piece, but he knew he would not work well by the light of the lamp. He needed sunshine to drive away the shadows.

He lighted the fire in his fireplace and sat down in his chair. Old Grouch did not join him. Puffing his pipe, Jerome caught himself listening for the return of the raccoons. After a while Mama came in. She ducked under the bed, and after a while she came out with a fat mouse between her teeth; she ate all of the mouse, fur and feet included. When she had finished her meal she washed her face and slicked her fur, giving careful attention to her long tail. Then she frisked about, doing stunts for Jerome. After playing for a while she left. Papa appeared within a few minutes. He, too, ducked under the bed, but he did not come out with a mouse. When he did come out he perched close to Jerome's feet and looked up at him eagerly.

"No luck?" Jerome asked.

Papa churred impatiently. Jerome got up and opened the cupboard. He set out milk and a slice of Spam. Papa went at his supper eagerly. Jerome glanced at the box in the corner. Old Grouch must be feeling very low not to be interested in the opening of a Spam can. It was the first time Jerome had been able to open a can of meat without having Old Grouch at his feet, demanding a portion.

Jerome smoked thoughtfully. The house was very still. Papa finished his meal and went outside to hunt for crickets. The four young raccoons did not come back. Jerome sighed. He knew he was sitting up waiting for them. Slowly the fire burned down until only a glow of light spread from it, not enough to reveal the red tracings in the face of the fireplace.

JEROME OPENED his eyes. Sunshine was coming in through the big window. Ever since coming to his home on the top of this hill Jerome had stayed in bed twenty minutes after waking up. It made him feel good to lie there lazy and warm, knowing he didn't have to leap out of bed and hurry into pants and shirt. No alarm clock wakened him. He didn't have to open the shop at seven. He turned on his side and looked at the yellow band of sunlight spread like a rug across the floor.

But this morning Jerome sat up at once. He looked around the room. Old Grouch was sitting in the sun by the window. He yawned lazily. Jerome sighed deeply. The youngsters had not returned. He swung his bare feet over the edge of the bed and sat wiggling his toes. Now that the young raccoons had done just what he had expected he felt sad. The place would be pretty quiet with only Old Grouch around.

"Just a couple of old bachelors," he said.

Old Grouch grumbled an answer. He was impatient with Jerome for not moving faster. He was hungry and wanted his breakfast.

Jerome didn't hurry. He laced his boots, then he washed his face. Old Grouch marched around the room grumbling and scolding. Jerome rattled the frying pan and thumped the coffeepot. The feeling of emptiness in his house made him want to make a noise. He fried a strip of bacon and an egg for himself, and a strip of bacon and an egg for Old Grouch. As he ate he studied the figure he was chiseling out of the cream-colored stone. He knew it was going to be good, and the thought made him forget the lonesomeness of his house. A happy glow filled him. He was an artist who had created something.

He hurriedly finished breakfast and washed up the dishes. Then he set to work upon the figure again. Noon came and he did not notice. Old Grouch had wandered off into the woods and was not there to remind him when lunch time came. He worked steadily on into the afternoon. He was now adding the fine touches, a chip off there, a sliver removed here. He had caught the coy look Mrs. Grouch always lifted to him. He worked awhile on the lower lip, then got up and stepped back. People would look down at the headstone from about where he was standing. Yes, it was a fine piece of work. He set it against the wall and fell to studying it. There was the little lady peeping over the edge of her box at him. It was good.

Old Grouch came wandering across the meadow. His face wore a discouraged frown instead of the scowl which was usually there. He had searched far for his wife but had failed to find any of her tracks except very cold ones. He paused and looked at the stone figure, but Jerome could not tell whether he liked it or not, or whether he recognized the stone raccoon peeping over the edge of the rock. He marched into the cabin and began demanding lunch. Jerome went in and gave him some tinned meat, then made himself a sandwich and carried it outside where he could study the statue while he munched.

After a half-hour of looking at it he picked it up and carried it inside. He set it on the table and got the sheet of paper Emma Lou had written the inscription on. He was busily figuring a layout for the wording when a shadow darkened the doorway. He looked up and saw Donald Roger Cabot standing there. Jerome was startled, then he had a flustered feeling. He was expecting Emma Lou any minute now, and he had an idea she'd be packing Ben's rifle. Donald Roger stepped into the cabin. In spite of an attempt to appear bored, he showed quite a little interest as he looked around.

"You ought not to come here," Jerome said.

"I came up to pay you for the raccoon my dog killed," Donald said stiffly. He reached into his hip pocket and pulled out a billfold.

Jerome looked quickly toward the door. He wondered where the dog was. If Emma Lou came upon the dog there would be trouble. Donald Roger smiled coldly.

"I tied Strong Heart to a tree down the hill," he said.

Jerome's cheeks began to flush. The boy's manner and his offer to pay for the death of Mrs. Grouch stirred anger in him. "You can't pay for a thing like that," he said sharply. "And you better go before Emma Lou shows up."

Donald shrugged his shoulders. He looked around the cabin. The curving wall of shaggy bark held his attention, then he looked at the fireplace. "Nice fireplace," he said.

What he was thinking was that it was a much better fireplace than his father had had built for twelve hundred dollars.

Jerome stirred impatiently. He was worried and trying not to show it. Donald turned to the table.

"I didn't think you'd take pay for that raccoon," he

said. "But it's the thing to do, pay what you owe." He smiled at Jerome. "I guess you think I mean ten dollars or fifteen. Will a hundred make it square?"

"No," Jerome said. He wanted to shout the word, but kept his voice steady. "And you better go. I don't want to see you and your dog shot on my property."

Donald laughed. "Yes, she'd shoot my dog and she'd shoot me." He said it as though he was saying it was a nice day.

Jerome got to his feet. "Then why don't you get going?"

Donald was looking at the figure on the table. He bent forward. "Not bad at all," he said. Then he added, "It's good."

In spite of his worry and irritation Jerome was pleased. Now that he had created a fine piece of work he was eager to have someone see it and like it. "It's not finished yet," he said.

"A raccoon looking over a wall watching you," Donald said. "What is it for?"

"It's a headstone," Jerome said.

Donald turned and looked at Jerome. A puzzled frown formed on his lips. "No, not really?"

"That's what it is for," Jerome said.

Donald turned back to the figure. "I'll get some red

stone and you can do a dog's head for me. I'd like to have it for my room."

"I'm not doing any work for anybody," Jerome said.

"You're doing this for that redheaded brat, aren't you?" Donald asked.

"It goes on a grave," Jerome said.

Donald looked at Jerome again, this time with more interest. He was trying to figure Jerome out. The man was as odd as his house. He interested Donald very much.

Jerome was looking through the window. Suddenly his mouth closed into a tight line. Emma Lou was coming across the meadow. She had Ben's rifle tucked under her arm. "There she comes now," Jerome said.

Donald turned and looked out through the window. His air of bored laziness left him. "Golly," he said. "I can't let her catch me here." He looked around the room, seeking a back door.

"No way for you to get out." Jerome stepped to the door, thinking he might be able to get Emma Lou away from the house long enough for Donald to escape.

"Hello!" Emma Lou greeted him. "I'm all excited. Did you get it finished?" She was looking down at the rock chips scattered on the doorstone.

"Not yet," Jerome said without moving out of the doorway. He had a feeling he wouldn't be able to get

CHAPTER FIVE

her away from the house until he showed her the figure, and he couldn't reach it without stepping back into the house and letting her come in.

"I had trouble getting away. Cilly was washing, and

I always have to turn the wringer." She set the rifle against the wall. "And I had to get around Ben so I could borrow the rifle."

"It isn't loaded, is it?" Jerome asked anxiously.

"Sure," Emma Lou answered.

"Thought you might take a look in the woods. The young raccoons went off and haven't come back." As he spoke Jerome stepped out on the doorstone and looked down the slope. He expected Emma Lou to follow him. The news of the departure of the raccoons ought to make her forget the headstone.

"Soon as I have a peek at the lovely lady." She stepped past him quickly. From where she had been standing she could see the back of the figure through the window.

Jerome jumped, but he could not stop her, so he followed her into the house, nerving himself for the worst. Looking over her shoulder, he was relieved to see that Donald had vanished. He did not have to make more than one guess as to where he was. There were only two places, up the wide fireplace chimney or under the bed. Jerome was certain Donald was under the bed. He didn't believe the young man would try the chimney.

Emma Lou drew in her breath as she looked upon the figure. She clasped her hands. "Oh! Oh! It's beautiful! Just like Charmine! Why, she's smiling up at us."

Jerome beamed proudly. He didn't know what to say. Emma Lou moved about, looking at the statue from different angles, and talking eagerly all the time. Jerome began to blush like a little boy. Emma Lou tossed her hat on the floor and sank into a chair.

"I'll bet no raccoon ever had such a fine headstone," she said.

"Lucky I had a nice piece of stone left," Jerome said. He was still feeling flustered and shy. He sat down and fumbled in his pocket for his pipe. As he stuffed tobacco into the bowl he heard a noise under the bed. He glanced quickly at Emma Lou. She hadn't heard the noise. Her elbows were propped on the table, her chin was in her palms, and she was dreamily regarding the stone raccoon. Jerome lighted his pipe.

At that moment Papa appeared at the door. He had heard Emma Lou's voice and had roused himself out of a sound sleep to come and see if she had brought anything for him. He walked over to her, waving his plume and churring a warm welcome. Emma Lou reached down and scratched his head. Papa looked up at her. She hadn't brought anything for him. He cocked his head and listened intently. He had heard a faint sound under the bed, and sounds from there meant mice. With a swish of his tail he skipped across the floor and ducked under the bed.

Emma Lou laughed. "He'll be out in a minute with a mouse," she said. "He's a fast worker."

Jerome gripped his pipe. He had an idea things were going to start happening fast. Emma Lou returned to her

admiring of the figure on the table. Jerome kept an eye on the bed.

"Say!" Emma Lou burst out suddenly. "I forgot all about the little raccoons. When did they leave? And where is Old Grouch?" She had just noticed that Old Grouch was not in the cabin. He had ducked out when Donald entered.

"They left last night right after supper. Haven't been

back since," Jerome said. Out of the corners of his eyes Jerome was watching the blanket hanging over the edge of the bed. It was waving gently.

"I wish they didn't have to go out into the world." Emma Lou could not hide her disappointment. Then her lips tightened. "All the more reason for my bagging that Cabot dog."

"I don't think he'll bother up this way," Jerome said. He was beginning to squirm. His ears were strained for the sound of small feet stamping angrily. Unless young Cabot had iron nerves and sense enough to play dead, there would be an explosion.

At that moment they heard a dog barking outside. Emma Lou stiffened. The yelps and barks were rapidly coming closer. The dog seemed to be following a trail. Emma Lou jumped to her feet. "That dog!" she shouted.

A black form darted across the floor. Papa had heard the dog and was on his way to defend his family. Jerome caught Emma Lou's arm and held her back. "Wait," he said.

Emma Lou struggled to get away from him. She could see Strong Heart through the doorway. He was bounding up the path. Then she saw Papa marching down the path to meet the dog. Strong Heart was a society dog. He had killed a few cats and a few possums and one raccoon, mostly upon orders from his master, but, in the case of the cats, on his own. The black and white animal walking toward him looked somewhat like a cat; in fact, he was convinced it was a cat. It would turn and flee, but it had used poor judgment; it would never be able to get to a tree before he nabbed it.

Jerome pulled Emma Lou back a few feet. "Let Papa handle this," he said.

Emma Lou stopped pulling and started to grin. Papa had started stamping his feet and churring savagely. Then he did his handstand. Strong Heart let out a wild and eager yelp. This would be the easiest cat kill he had ever made. His mouth opened wide as he leaped to snap up the small black kitten. Papa's hind feet hit the path, and like a cowboy facing a badman, he fanned his gun and fired. Strong Heart's wild yelp changed to a stifled gurgle, which was followed by a wheezing gulp. He hit the path with all four feet planted and digging frantically. The wheezing gulp was followed by a loud roar of anguish. Strong Heart did a remarkable reverse. His big feet dug at the path as he lunged away toward the woods.

Emma Lou and Jerome dived out into the open as a wave of highly scented air rolled into the house. Emma Lou caught up her rifle as she ran. She darted into the meadow, with Jerome close behind her. When they were in the clear they stood and held their sides and laughed.

Strong Heart had looked so foolish. Finally Emma Lou said:

"You'll have to move out for a while."

Jerome nodded. "If Papa could have taken him on down the hill a little way instead of right at the door." Then he chuckled. He was thinking about Donald under the bed.

Emma Lou started off down the hill. "If I hurry I may get a shot at that dog," she said.

Jerome didn't think she'd catch even a glimpse of Strong Heart. The dog had been traveling fast when he entered the woods, and he had been taking a straight course for home. But he was glad Emma Lou was leaving for a little while. He had to get rid of Donald.

Emma Lou began to run. She ducked into the woods like an Indian. Picking up Strong Heart's trail was an easy matter. Even Emma Lou's feeble powers of smell were enough.

Jerome turned toward his house. Donald burst forth, holding his nose. He staggered over to Jerome and released his nose. "Phooey!" he burst out. "Do you keep skunks too?"

"I have seven," Jerome said with a grin.

"Seven?" Donald Roger looked startled. "I saw only one. The darned thing licked the end of my nose."

"This is the first time it's happened. Your dog trailed

you up here and tried to kill the skunk." Jerome was still grinning.

Donald returned the grin. "For a while I thought it was going to be me. I kept still and let him look me over." He shrugged his shoulders.

"I don't think your dog will ever bother another skunk," Jerome said.

"When he gets back from the dry cleaner's he'll be locked up, I know that." Donald started away. "I don't smell so good myself."

"I wouldn't go that way," Jerome said. "Emma Lou is down there with her rifle."

"So what?" Donald called over his shoulder. He walked into the woods without looking back.

Jerome waited and listened. A wind sprang up and blew the musky odor away from the cabin. Jerome walked to his house. There really wasn't any damage done. Papa was standing just outside the ventilator hole. He beamed up at Jerome. Papa did not seem to have a bit of scent on himself. He was standing guard, and it was easy to see he was all puffed up over his victory.

Jerome sat down and lighted his pipe. The smoke might help if the wind changed. The wind did not change. He did not hear any shots on the slope below. After a while Emma Lou came back.

"See him?" Jerome asked.

"No. He ran like a deer." Emma Lou set the rifle against the wall. "I guess Papa did a better job than I could have done," she said.

The wind suddenly shifted and they had to make a hasty retreat. Jerome looked at his house and frowned. "Guess I'll have to camp out for a while," he said.

Emma Lou helped him fix camp under a tree a short distance from the house. Jerome knew nothing at all about making camp, but Emma Lou knew everything. She dug a fire pit and fixed a pine-bough bed for him. She nailed a box to a tree for a cupboard. They brought blankets and supplies from the house. When the camp was finished Jerome was tickled with it. During the summer there was never any rain. He would be snug and he would be roughing it in the open for the first time. The idea appealed to him; it made him feel rugged. He would live like the pioneers.

CHAPTER SIX

A WEEK OF camping out under the big oak tree made Jerome appreciate his house. He got four wood ticks on him, all burrowed into him so deeply he had to dig them out with his penknife; he caught a cold which gave him the sniffles. His stomach got upset because he did not know how to cook over a campfire. A possum stole all of his bacon and his eggs. Jerome was glad to move back into his house. There was only a lingering smell of musk in his front yard.

The headstone was lettered and in place. Emma Lou admired it very much.

The first thing Jerome did when he got back into his house was to heat a tub of water and take a bath. He smeared the tick bites with salve, shaved, and felt very good. Old Grouch was glad to have him move back. He had never seen any reason for moving out in the first place. He had slept in his box every night, but he had

had to visit the camp for food. He was as fat as ever, but Jerome thought he was pining for his wife. He did not go off looking for another mate. Jerome pampered him and put up with his grumbling.

Emma Lou roamed the woods with Ben's rifle, but she never saw Donald or Strong Heart. She was sure she had won a complete victory. She did not know that Donald had sworn to have his revenge. Nothing had happened because he had not figured out a way to get even. Strong Heart was no longer allowed to run in the woods. He had been sent to an animal hospital for descenting. Upon his return he was confined to the fenced yard.

Donald had visited Jerome's hill a number of times and had seen Emma Lou on patrol without her suspecting he was watching. Emma Lou would have doubled her efforts had she known he wasn't staying off the mountain.

Jerome soon realized that he wasn't going to stop using his stonecutter's tools now that he had started again. He had an itch to do something else, not a headstone; he didn't ever want to make another tombstone. He finally selected a slab of rock and started upon a small statue. He decided to make a statue of Old Grouch. Working on it gave him a good feeling, and when he had the head roughed out he knew it was going to look like

Old Grouch. Emma Lou was excited about it, so excited he decided he'd give it to her when it was finished.

Toward the middle of August, Papa and Mama brought the children into the house. They came marching in through the little door, Mama first, then the five little ones, then Papa. The children were very much like

their parents, only smaller. Mama led a grand march around the room before they gathered in the center of the floor. Papa sat up and looked at Jerome proudly.

It was clear to Jerome that Papa was going to expect a lot of help from him in feeding this family. They were now at an age when they wanted to eat all of the time but were not able to hunt. Jerome knew he would accept the job. He set out two saucers of condensed milk and a plate of meat scraps. The little skunks lapped up the milk and ate all of the scraps. No coaxing was needed to get them to try a new kind of food, and none of them had to be scolded for not eating.

Old Grouch gave the skunk family a wide berth. He hopped up on a chair and sat watching them. Papa kept an eye on him, though by now he had come to consider Old Grouch a part of the fixtures in the house, like the chairs and the table and the bed. But he did not intend that the old raccoon should forget his place and try to nip any of the children.

Emma Lou took the skunk family over as soon as they started leaving the nest. Jerome wondered if they would decide to take up quarters in the house. They did not. If the chimney had not been in use every night they would have taken it over gladly, but they did not like the open room. They liked a dark spot to sleep during the day. They considered Emma Lou a very special friend and would do anything to please her. One afternoon she announced that she was going to stay for supper. She had never sat before the fireplace. She would light it and sit before the fire with Jerome after supper. Her real reason was that she wanted to play with the skunks. They were at their best after dark, and she wouldn't have to coax them out from under the floor.

"Sure your family won't worry?" Jerome asked.

"Job and Cilly are in the city. The boys are all up at the wood camp. There's nobody home to worry." Emma Lou smiled.

Jerome grinned. He always thought it funny when she spoke of her mother and father as Job and Cilly. He rather liked the idea, but it wasn't something he was used to.

Emma Lou helped with the supper things. She was eager to light the fire in the fireplace, but she waited until the dishes were washed and stacked away. Old Grouch ate a huge supper from what was left over. When he sat down beside his plate his stomach hid his feet from view.

"You'll have to get his statue done before he gets so fat it won't look like him," Emma Lou said.

"Not much more to do," Jerome said.

They moved to the fireplace. Emma Lou held a match under the shavings. The flame grew until it licked around the big logs. Seating herself on the hearth, she pulled her knees up and locked her arms around them. Old Grouch waddled over and sat on the other side of the hearth. Jerome sat in his chair and puffed on his pipe.

"Have to cut some lettering on the base," Jerome said.

"What will you put on it?"

"Just 'Old Grouch,' " Jerome said with a grin.

Emma Lou stared thoughtfully into the fire. The light made her hair look coppery. It outlined her tipped-up nose and her small chin. Jerome thought he'd like to do a piece of work like that. He thought he would try it sometime. Emma Lou had been considering a nicer name to cut into the base of the statue. She couldn't think of any name that fitted the old raccoon better than the one Jerome had given him.

The seven little skunks came in for their milk. They disappointed Emma Lou by staying only a little while after they had finished their supper. Papa and Mama were giving the little skunks night lessons. A well-schooled skunk needed to know his way about after dark. Night was their hunting time. She tried to coax them into playing with her, but Papa and Mama were firm. They marched their brood out through the little door. Emma Lou returned to the hearth and sat down. Old Grouch burped a couple of times, then dropped off into a sound sleep.

"This is wonderful," Emma Lou said. "When I grow up I'm going to have a cabin just like this. Will you build my fireplace for me?"

"Sure," Jerome agreed. Then he frowned. "But don't you want other things more than a house in the woods?"

"I did have other plans," Emma Lou admitted. She

blushed as she remembered what those plans had been. They seemed sort of silly now. A tall knight on a white horse, a castle, and all that. A house like this would be nicer. "I've decided I'll have a cabin like this one. The other house"—she did not say castle—"was a lot bigger, but not nearly so nice."

Suddenly Old Grouch cocked an ear and opened one eye. Then he opened the other eye and sat up. He sniffed and chuckled deeply. Then he lifted his muzzle and gave a low "Whoo-oo-oo." Jerome and Emma Lou looked at him in surprise.

"Why, he hasn't sung a note since she died," Jerome said. He paused and looked toward the little door. It had opened and a furry head was poked into the room.

They both turned to watch the little door. A raccoon walked into the cabin, followed by a smaller raccoon. It was the Slick One, and he had a little lady with him. The small raccoon seemed nervous, but the Slick One just shoved her toward the center of the floor. They both sat down and looked around the room.

"He's brought home a bride," Jerome said.

"Here come two more," Emma Lou whispered.

The little door opened and another pair marched in. They were closely followed by a third pair. The six raccoons sat down in a circle, and three of them looked eagerly up at Jerome, who had gotten to his feet and was standing beside the bed. "They came back married," Emma Lou said, and then she giggled.

The strange raccoons looked scared and ready to bolt for the door, but Old Grouch's children were not afraid.

"Runt didn't come back," Jerome said.

Before Emma Lou could answer, the door opened and in popped Runt. She was followed by a burly fellow as big as Old Grouch himself. She sat down in the circle, and he sat down beside her.

Old Grouch waddled down off the hearth and walked over to his family. He stood looking them over for a while, then he sat down beside Runt's husband, and he, too, looked up at Jerome. Nine pairs of bright eyes regarded him; nine faces beamed.

Jerome grinned at them. He wanted to laugh, but he was afraid that might scare the strangers away. He moved slowly to the cupboard and pulled a string. Nine heads turned to follow his movements. It was clear the strange brides and bridegrooms had been informed of what to expect. It was also plain to be seen that they were skeptical. Jerome fixed little squares of meat on a big platter. He added some bits of crackers and dry toast. He set the tray down inside the circle and went to his chair.

"Runt copped the prize of the season," Emma Lou said. "I had a hunch she would."

"She's a smart one," Jerome agreed. "Always was smart."

"Wonder if they'd run away if I tried to join them?" Emma Lou asked.

"If they do they'll come back. They've had a taste of that meat," Jerome said.

Emma Lou got up and walked toward the circle. The four wild raccoons stopped eating and stared at her. Suddenly Runt's burly husband broke and made a dash for the door. He went out with the three others close upon his tail. Emma Lou sat down and started talking to raccoons. They ate hungrily, but they were polite enough to pay attention to what she said.

Very soon a furry face appeared at the door. Runt's mate peeked in. He watched the raccoons feasting at the platter for a minute, then he barged in and joined them, shoving in at Runt's side. The other three followed. Once they were back at the banquet, they did not seem afraid of Emma Lou.

Emma Lou looked up at Jerome and laughed. "Before the rains come you'll have twenty-five or thirty raccoons to share your house with you."

The idea startled Jerome. But Emma Lou was right. He wondered what would happen a year from today. He did a bit of arithmetic and figured he'd have more than a hundred raccoons within a year's time. He had no doubt now that they would all stay with him. He had a feeling they would all demand food.

"Hard to tell what may happen," he said cautiously.

"You'll have a houseful of raccoons, that's what will happen." Emma Lou sighed. "I wish Charmine could see them. She'd sure be proud of her children."

Jerome frowned. He was wondering if he wouldn't have to chase them away. Emma Lou seemed to read his thoughts.

"You won't have to chase them away, and they won't leave. I'll help you make nests for them."

"I don't know," Jerome said.

"It will be wonderful." Emma Lou was enthusiastic.

"I'll have to make nests. If I don't there won't be a pound of stuffing left in my mattress." Jerome shook his head. He was remembering how Mrs. Grouch had helped herself to the stuffing in his mattress. "I could donate this mattress to them and buy me a new one."

"There's an old one in our attic. I'll put the pack saddle on Frank and bring it up tomorrow. They won't steal the stuffing while you are in bed."

"I wouldn't be too sure," Jerome said doubtfully.

"You wait and see," Emma Lou assured him.

A half-hour later Runt led her mate over to the box in the corner. She left while the others were still picking up the few crumbs left on the platter. Old Grouch was already in the box. She hopped right in on top of him. He made a lot of noise and some fur flew as they tussled in the box. It was Old Grouch who got out, and he moved fast for one so fat.

Emma Lou and Jerome laughed. Runt was coyly coaxing her burly mate into the box. He was keeping one eye on Old Grouch and hanging back. Old Grouch turned his back on the pair. He marched to the fireplace and sat down. From the elevation of the hearth he delivered an angry tirade at his children and his in-laws.

"Runt will get along," Emma Lou said. "But I have to be running on home."

"You've been expecting this to happen?" Jerome asked.

"I had a pretty good idea what was going on," Emma Lou admitted. "I've seen them all out in the woods getting it planned. But I was just lucky in picking tonight to sit here by the fire."

Jerome got to his feet. He smiled at her. He was sure she had been keeping a close watch over the raccoons and hoping this would happen. He thought she might even have had something to do with their home-coming, but he didn't mention it.

The night was dark except for pale starlight, but Emma Lou had a flashlight. It was a big and powerful light belonging to Ben, a light he sometimes used for purposes he did not talk about and which the local game warden would have considered very bad. Ben had taken his rifle with him to the wood camp, but Emma Lou was not afraid. There was nothing to be afraid of.

As she moved along the trail she did not flash the light. She could see well enough to get along. If she moved silently and without a light she would hear many night sounds she was interested in. She knew a mountain lion had drifted up along the ridge and was paying the mountain a visit. She also knew that a cougar was harmless so far as man went. Cougars knew they had no business bothering any of man's tribe. Any cougar who managed to live did it in spite of men with traps and guns who were all eager to kill his kind. Emma Lou had tried to catch a glimpse of this cougar. Ben had told her that a lion would follow a person out of curiosity. If he did she might be able to flash her light on him and get a good look at him.

So she moved along carelessly, whistling softly. She hoped Ben was right about lions having a big bump of curiosity. She whistled, but she also listened carefully, and she didn't look back along the trail. According to Ben, if you looked back the cougar would make off in a hurry; he'd know you knew he was trailing you. Once or twice she was sure she heard the padding of big feet on the trail behind her. But each time when she slowed her pace she heard nothing except the usual night sounds: the crickets, the rustle of a wood mouse, the hoot of an owl. Once she was startled by the sharp bark of a gray fox close to the trail, but deep in a thicket. She whistled at him, and he answered sharply before making off. She could hear loose stones slithering down a bank as he scurried away.

She came to a stop where the trail curved around a dell choked with woodwardia ferns. It was a spring gulch where the ground stayed wet all summer and the huge ferns grew higher than her head. Below the fern dell was a meadow which was almost flat. Emma Lou knew that a doe had a late fawn hidden in the ferns, but she did not pause for a peep at the fawn. If a lion was following her she certainly wasn't going to lead him to the baby black-tail. If she kept right on, the lion would never know because a baby deer has no scent at all when it is very young.

She was just below the fern dell when she heard a low snarl, then a bleating scream. The sounds came from the meadow. Emma Lou halted and gripped her flashlight. The throaty snarl had been deep and terrifying. She was sure it had been made by a lion. It sent a chill racing up her spine, and for a minute she wanted to run away. The bleating cry sounded again. It was even worse than the snarl; it was filled with terror.

Suddenly she knew what was happening. The cougar was attacking the doe, who had been feeding out in the meadow.

Anger flared up in her, and she did not stop to consider what she ought to do or what was safe to do. She just gripped her flashlight and started off the trail and down a little slope toward the meadow. She struggled through a mass of blackberry vines, and after a half dozen steps she came to the edge of the meadow. Shooting the powerful beam of Ben's hunting light out across the meadow, she picked out a tawny shape. She steadied the light, and it revealed a lank cougar. He had the doe gripped by the neck. She was down and half turned over. He was tearing at her neck savagely. When the light hit him he leaped back from the doe and faced Emma Lou. His yellow eyes glared horribly. He snarled as loud as any zoo lion and lashed his tail. Emma Lou held the light on him. She was trying to yell, but she wasn't able to make a sound. The lion stood his ground for half a minute, then he whirled and bounded away. She stabbed the beam of light after him, holding it on him. Before he outran the light he was making twenty-foot leaps.

Emma Lou stood where she was for a long time, and she didn't turn off the light. The lion certainly had not looked like the cowardly beast Ben had said it would be.

She shifted the light back to the doe. The doe lay in a heap, and Emma Lou had a dreadful feeling that she was dead. Finally she moved out across the meadow to where the doe lay. Her eyes were open, but she was dead. Her throat had been slashed open, and her neck seemed to be twisted, possibly broken.

She remembered the fawn, and panic seized her. She was sure the cougar would come back. He was probably sitting well outside the reach of her flashlight, waiting until she went away. He might even be creeping toward her through the tall grass. She headed for the fern dell and did not turn off the flashlight. Her probing light found the fawn. Its big eyes stared at her from under a frond. Emma Lou moved in. She got the fawn into her arms. The little fellow did not kick or struggle. It snuggled against her and tried to pretend it was dead or asleep. After a tough struggle she got back on the trail. She stood for a minute considering what to do, then headed upward toward Jerome's house.

Jerome was seated in his chair before the fire when Emma Lou pushed open his door. She staggered into the room and set the fawn down on the floor. Its legs curled under it, and it settled down, stretching out its neck and laying back its ears as it flattened itself against the boards. Jerome had been drowsing. He started and leaned forward, blinking his eyes, not quite sure he was seeing what he did see. There was wild scurrying and dim shapes darted from under the bed, from corners of the room, and out of the boxes. The fire had died down, so there was only a rosy glow of light in the room. In less than a minute all of the raccoons were outside except Old Grouch and Runt, who stayed in her nest even when her burly mate fled.

"Well, well," was all Jerome could say as he stood looking at the fawn.

Emma Lou was so out of breath she could not explain for a few minutes. She sank down on the floor and began stroking the fawn's neck. The baby deer was no bigger than a large rabbit. Its spots showed clearly, but the rest of it blended with the floor so that Jerome seemed to be seeing only spots. He didn't ask any questions. He had got over being surprised at anything Emma Lou did. She looked up at him and sighed deeply.

"A lion killed its mother. He'll kill this baby, too, if we don't keep it here," she explained.

"Lion?" Jerome repeated. He had no idea there were lions on his mountain. He thought she was talking about the only kind of lion he had ever seen, a great beast with a tawny mane.

"A mountain lion," Emma Lou explained. "Ben saw him, and he's going to hunt him when he gets done with the wood."

"You started home with a lion loose in the woods?" Jerome stared at her in astonishment.

"They won't hurt a person." She frowned. "In a way it's my fault. I talked Ben into waiting to hunt the lion. I wanted to see him alive in the woods."

Jerome opened his mouth, then closed it without saying anything. He shook his head. Looking down at the fawn, he said, "Well, well."

"You can keep it here tonight. After I milk Bess and Pinky in the morning I'll bring up some milk for it. We'll have to bottle-feed it." She leaned forward and rubbed her head against the neck of the little fawn. "Poor baby," she whispered. "You'll be snug and safe here."

"You can't walk down that trail alone," Jerome said firmly. "We should have a gun." He looked about the room for a weapon. "You had better stay here tonight," he added.

"I should go home," Emma Lou said. "One of the boys might come down from the camp."

Jerome took a deep breath. "I guess you should go home. I'll walk down with you." The minute he spoke Jerome regretted it, but he didn't try to squirm out.

Emma Lou didn't refuse to let him go with her. Now that she had time to think it over she was scared. Jerome saw she was frightened, and it did not make him feel happy. He had only a vague idea what a mountin lion looked like. All he could recall in the way of lions were those he had seen in the zoo. He remembered how the brutes acted at feeding time. He wet his lips and tried to manage a smile.

"I don't think it's a very big lion," Emma Lou said. "It ran away when I flashed the light in its face. Ben says all mountain lions are cowards."

Jerome shuddered. His regard for Emma Lou's courage bounced upward. She had walked up to a lion and flashed her light into its face. He couldn't let her see that his knees were knocking together. "I'll pull on my boots," he said. "Guess the deer will be safe until I get back."

As he laced his boots Jerome wondered what he could take along as a weapon. He finally decided he would take his stone mason's hammer, the heavy one with the long handle. At any rate, he knew how to use it, and he wouldn't have known how to use a gun.

Emma Lou moved the fawn over into a corner and covered it with one of Jerome's coats. Jerome armed himself with the heavy hammer, and they started out.

The trip down the trail was not marred by sight or sound of the lion. When they were opposite the scene of the kill Emma Lou shot her light out across the meadow. The carcass of the doe lay in the grass, but there was no

sign of the lion. The lion was at that instant swinging along a ridge five miles away. He was alive because he was wary and very careful. He was heading away from the place where he had been spotted by a human being.

When they reached the Eppy house Emma Lou gave Jerome the flashlight. She felt just a little bit ashamed of herself now that they had covered the trail and the lion had not been seen or heard.

"I'll be up after I milk the cows," she said. "We have to save that baby deer."

Jerome nodded. He wasn't worrying about the fawn. It was safe in his house. He was worrying about the trip back up the trail. He did not know that the lion was far away. He was sure it was hiding along the trail. He climbed as fast as he could. For once he did not take an easy pace with plenty of stops along the way. He kept shooting his light along the back trail, and off to the sides and up ahead. He heard quite a few sounds which could have been made by a lion, and once his light picked out a pair of glaring eyes. When the eyes appeared he froze in his tracks. They were very close and looked very big. Not being able to whirl and run gave him time to see what sort of beast the eyes belonged to. The light revealed the form of a fat possum. The light had blinded it so that it could not run away. As soon as Jerome shifted the beam the possum went blundering off through the brush.

After that Jerome moved faster. He was puffing and his face was red when he finally reached his house. He got inside and would have barred the door if there had been any bar. He snapped the flimsy latch shut and stood looking at the door. He was glad he had made the little door so small a lion could not squeeze through it.

Jerome tossed a few small pieces of wood on the bed of coals in the fireplace. When the flames leaped up he saw that all of the raccoons had come back and were sleeping here and there about the room. The fawn was asleep under his coat. None of the brides had taken the trouble to raid his mattress. That would come later on when they got to thinking about families. Old Grouch poked his head out from under the bed. He had pulled a pair of Jerome's pants off a hook and wadded them up for a bed. Runt peeped over the edge of her box. She reminded Jerome of her mother. He smiled at her and she gave him a coy look before she snuggled down beside her husband.

When Jerome went to his bed he found one pair of raccoons on it. He moved them to the floor, where they sat blinking and looking abused as he undressed and got ready for bed. Before he dropped off to sleep he decided it was time he gave some thought to his household problems. They were piling up on him fast. But he was too sleepy to figure out what he ought to do. Tomorrow he would do some figuring. He sighed deeply and dropped off to sleep.

CHAPTER SEVEN

MORNING dawned bright and sunshiny. Jerome was awakened by the bleating of the fawn. The young one was hungry and wanted its mother. Jerome tossed aside the blankets and sat up. For a half minute he did not know what had wakened him. Then he remembered what had happened the night before. There had been a lion and Emma Lou had brought a baby deer into the house to save it. The baby deer bleated loudly. Its head appeared over the edge of his bed. Two big ears waved at him and two big eyes regarded him.

Jerome pulled up his knees. He sat looking at the hungry fawn. Things were getting out of hand in his house. He was playing host to nine raccoons, seven skunks, and this baby deer. The raccoons and the skunks were a problem he could handle. The fawn worried him. It was like having a baby left on his doorstep. Jerome knew nothing at all about babies. He got some comfort out of thinking that Emma Lou would be along presently, and she would know what to do.

He slid his feet over the side of the bed. The fawn jumped back and stared at the feet, then it lunged forward and tried to get one of Jerome's toes into its mouth. Jerome jerked his feet back up on the bed. He escaped by going over the foot, but the fawn came nuzzling after him the moment his feet hit the floor. Jerome managed to keep it away while he got dressed, but he had several wet spots on his pants and shirt before he managed to get his boots laced. He sat down and held the hungry fawn away from him. He didn't see how he was going to be able to cook breakfast. The raccoons were sitting around waiting, their eyes fixed upon Jerome.

Emma Lou arrived with a bottle and a jug of milk just as Jerome was getting ready to flee from his house. She was beaming and full of good spirits. The fawn deserted Jerome at once. Emma Lou fixed a bottle of milk after Jerome got the fire started and water hot so the milk could be warmed. The fawn drank three bottles of milk, then it allowed Emma Lou to put it to bed in the corner under Jerome's coat.

Jerome cooked breakfast. He felt better now that he knew what to do about the fawn. You just gave it a quart of milk and it went to sleep. It seemed quite simple. But he thought it might be better off with Emma Lou.

"You could handle it better," he suggested.

Emma Lou shook her head. "It wouldn't be safe down at our place. We have three hounds. They'd tear it to bits; anyway, they'd chase it. The boys let them chase deer."

Jerome nodded. She did not have to go into the matter of the Eppy hounds chasing deer. Jerome already knew the nine Eppys—anyway, eight of them—liked venison and ate quite a bit of it. He also knew that catching a black-tail was best accomplished with dogs. On several occasions Jerome had met a strange man prowling through his timber, heading over into the wild country above the Eppy farm. The man had talked to him once, and Jerome had learned he was a game warden. The warden had asked a lot of questions about the Eppys and their hounds. He had told the warden nothing. He did not know anything for sure, though he suspected the Eppy boys did a bit of hunting out of season. Because they never poached on his land he could truthfully say he had never seen them running deer with their hounds.

After agreeing to keep the fawn Jerome realized he had made a mistake. For one thing, he soon learned that the baby deer was always hungry. It followed him everywhere; he couldn't take a step without feeling its wet nose on the seat of his pants, and it had a way of butting him with its head when he did not respond to its wet muzzle with a bottle of milk. It made odd sounds, and its ears flapped constantly, and its stump tail flapped faster than its ears. It bounced when it walked, and sometimes it got so pepped up its antics made Jerome dizzy. In desperation he finally took the matter up with Emma Lou.

"He's a pest," he said. "He won't let me sit down for a minute."

Emma Lou was sympathetic. Jerome did look frazzled, and she was sorry for him, but she was sure that if they turned the fawn loose in the woods it would fall prey to a bobcat or a coyote. The lion might come back any day. She finally got an idea.

"We'll build a little corral back of your cabin," she said.

Jerome considered this and finally nodded his approval. He should have thought of that himself. He wouldn't mind having the fawn if it was in a little corral. He'd be glad to feed it when Emma Lou wasn't around. He really liked the little scamp. He had never seen a creature more lovable.

"We'll make a fence just so high." Emma Lou held up a hand just even with her nose. "When he's big enough to jump over a fence that high he'll be big enough to live in the woods by himself."

Jerome beamed. He was relaxing in his chair. The only chance he got to relax was when Emma Lou was there to take the fawn away from him. He wouldn't want to keep the deer after it had grown big enough to go off into the woods. "Will the lion bother him in an open pen?" he asked.

"No." Emma Lou was sure of it. She might have said that she was sure the lion had moved on to other fields. She and Ben had spent a lot of time looking for the lion. Ben wanted the skin for a rug. He was sure the lion had moved on, and Ben wouldn't be mistaken. And she knew that if the lion ever did come back Ben would be after him and get him.

She didn't tell Jerome this. She had an idea he might want to turn the fawn loose, and she wanted to keep it where she could play with it. She planned to teach it tricks; possibly she could work it into the circus she was planning. She had the seven skunks already doing tricks, and she was making headway with the raccoons.

She had sawed a bay-tree limb into small cylinders, one little cylinder for each skunk. The skunks quickly learned to hop up on their perches and sit with their paws folded over their stomachs. They were always rewarded by bits of meat. They were so eager to do their trick that they always ran to the little cylinders and hopped up on them as soon as they came into the cabin.

Jerome found himself getting interested in the circus idea. He had never interfered with the lives of his friends or tried to shape them; he had just lived with them. But they seemed so willing to learn tricks that it did not seem wrong to teach them to do stunts. He did not have Emma Lou's patience, but he was able to help her in some ways. The raccoon trick she worked out was based upon their curiosity. No raccoon could pass a crack or a cranny or a hole without reaching into it to see if anything was hidden there. Nor could they pass any bright or shining object without stopping to examine it. Emma Lou used bits of abalone shell in her trick. It was a game of hide the shell, and the raccoons soon learned to play it. Emma Lou tried hard to make the raccoons understand that the one finding the most bits of shell would win a prize. She never got it through their heads. Runt usually found the most shell bits, but when she sat up to receive the prize the others all crowded around and sat up, too, their heads cocked on one side, their bright eyes watching eagerly. Emma Lou always ended up by dividing the prize, which was usually jelly beans, until she discovered that they liked canned corn better. They were not particular about food; they ate frogs, meat, sardines, nuts, fruit, and vegetables. They loved crickets and grasshoppers, but Emma Lou wouldn't kill a cricket, and she didn't care to stuff her pockets with grasshoppers because their habit of spitting tobacco juice made them messy.

Now that they had decided upon making a pen for the fawn Emma Lou was eager to get at it. She and Jerome started cutting saplings and hauling them to the house. Jerome started making the fence while she went on cutting saplings.

It was the sapling cutting that got Donald interested in what was going on. He had become expert at scouting Jerome's woods. At first he was only bent upon revenge. Then curiosity made him start watching the cabin. He got interested in the seven skunks and the nine raccoons.

There was a lot he could not see because it went on inside the cabin, but the animals often frolicked with their friends outside the house. Once Emma Lou did the skunk trick out on the doorstone, and the shell game was often played outdoors. Donald was fascinated. He was still angry with Emma Lou, but he was also sorry he wasn't welcome at the Kildee house. It would have been fun teaching the animals tricks.

When the fawn arrived Donald got an idea, and when they started working on the corral he was sure it was a good idea.

Jerome and Emma Lou were so busy they did not suspect they were being watched, or that anyone was plotting against them. Once the pen got under way, Jerome decided there ought to be a little shed set against the redwood tree so the fawn would have a snug place to sleep. He built a shed and thatched the roof with bark and dirt. He made a small gate for the corral. He really let his imagination work on that gate. He decorated it with circles of green willow and with diamonds of red madroña. The deep mahogany color of the barkless madroña contrasted nicely with the pale green bark of the willow. It was a really fine gate.

Emma Lou spent so much time at Jerome's place that Cilly finally asked Ben to wander up there just to see what was going on. Ben picked a time when Emma Lou was not there. He dropped in on Jerome while Jerome was darning a red sock. When he appeared at the door a small commotion broke loose inside the house. The raccoons all dashed out between his legs. Ben grinned broadly and said, "Hello."

"Hello," Jerome replied. "I guess you're Ben."

Ben nodded. He had pulled off his black hat and was hunching over so he would not bump his head when he entered.

"Come in," Jerome invited.

Ben came in and sat down in the chair by the table. He dropped his hat on the floor and looked around the cabin.

"You got quite a batch of critters around here," he said with a broad grin.

"They come and go," Jerome said.

"Emmy said you had plenty, but I never reckoned you had such a flock." Ben was already satisfied that Emma Lou was safe up here at Jerome's place.

"She's a fine girl," Jerome said. "She has the skunks

doing tricks. You'll have to come up some evening and have her show you the skunk tricks."

"Skunks?" Ben stopped grinning.

"Seven of them, and she can make them do most anything she wants," Jerome said proudly. "Smart little tykes."

"That's sure interestin'," Ben said. "I never fooled none with skunks. Never made no sets for 'em."

"They're smart, just as smart as the raccoons," Jerome said. He laid the mended sock on the bed. "How about some coffee, Ben?"

"Don't mind if I do," Ben said. "But skunks, any I ever knew was dumb and plumb touchy."

"These are little spotted skunks, not at all like the ones we used to have around the swamps. Playful little fellows." Jerome chuckled. "Always playing pranks on the raccoons."

"I never paid them much mind," Ben said. "Always figured a skunk was a skunk. I'll sure come up with Emma some evening." He fished out a stubby pipe and began looking for tobacco in his pockets. Jerome passed his jar of tobacco across to Ben. Ben sniffed the tobacco and smiled. It was a bit better mixture than Job bought.

They smoked with their coffee. Ben drank three cups. He liked it black, but he used plenty of sugar. When he stood up to leave he said:

"Any time I can lend a hand, jest holler."

Jerome knew Ben meant it. He liked Ben and he had a feeling Ben liked him. He had an idea Ben had been sent up to see what was going on, but he didn't let on.

Ben walked away whistling a tune. He was a big man, even if he was only seventeen years old. Jerome watched him as he swung across the meadow. Ben was the smallest of the Eppy men, but that didn't make him small compared with most men. Jerome went back to his mending. He was using a potato for a mending ball. A potato made a good darning ball. You could pick one the right size to fit your sock, a long one if the hole was in the heel, a round one if it was in the toe. He finished the last sock. Getting to his feet, he pulled a button. When a drawer opened he dropped the potato into it. Raccoons liked potatoes and would steal it if he left it out.

Emma Lou arrived and Jerome went out to watch her feed the little deer. The fawn was costing the Eppys quite a bit of milk, but Emma Lou did the milking, so she was the only one who really knew about it. And the cows were supposed to drop off in their milk during the summer months when there was no green grass.

The fawn nudged the gate eagerly, its tail doing a

crazy dance. Emma Lou opened the gate and stepped into the corral. She had taught the fawn to drink out of the bucket, so feeding was not so much of a problem now. Jerome leaned on the fence. Emma Lou clutched the bucket tightly so the fawn could not butt it over. It never seemed to learn that a pail did not need butting to let its milk down.

Emma Lou looked up at Jerome. "I've been thinking," she said.

Jerome nodded. He waited to hear what she had been thinking, hoping it was not an idea for adding some more animals to his household.

"He has to have a name." She patted the silky back of the little buck. "How about Monarch?"

Jerome looked at the little fellow. He was recalling a picture he had once seen on a calendar. He had kept it tacked on his shop wall over his workbench. It was a picture of a regal stag poised on top of a cliff. The title under the picture had read: MONARCH OF ALL HE SURVEYS. He grinned. It seemed hardly likely the little buck would ever grow to look like that stag. He thought Emma Lou had seen the picture; possibly the Eppys had received one of those calendars. He nodded seriously. Naming him Monarch would give him something to shoot at.

"Nice name," he said.

Monarch chose that moment to give a big butt. Milk splashed up into Emma Lou's face, leaving a white blob of foam on her nose.

"Monarch!" she said sharply. "You'll be sorry if you spill your milk."

Monarch butted again, but Emma Lou was ready for him. She eased the bucket backward, and no damage was done. Jerome lighted his pipe. He felt lazy, like relaxing and having himself a nap, but he knew Emma Lou would have things she wanted to do.

"We have to make some changes in the raccoon nests," he said, thinking he might as well get something easy started. "The pair under the stove argued and quarreled with Runt and her hubby all night. Kept me awake until daylight."

Emma Lou took the bucket away from Monarch. He shoved a dripping muzzle against her knee and started sucking lustily. Emma Lou shoved him back and ducked through the gate.

"It's Runt," she said. "She loves to pick a quarrel with the others, and she never knows when to quit. I wish I understood raccoon talk; I'd like to know what she says to the others to get them so riled up. I might be able to use it when school starts this fall." She grinned at Jerome.

"She picks a fight, and then she gets behind that big

husband of hers." Jerome grinned broadly. "She's making a regular bully out of him."

"If Old Grouch was any good he'd teach them something," Emma Lou said. "But he's just plain lazy."

"He's sort of lost his grip," Jerome admitted.

They went into the cabin to study the problem. The raccoons were all sleeping except Old Grouch, who seemed to be suffering from an attack of insomnia. He was wandering about with a sad look on his face, grunting and mumbling to himself. He couldn't sleep well at night because he was a raccoon, and now he wasn't able to sleep in the daytime. He hadn't lost any weight, which meant he wasn't really suffering much. But Jerome felt sorry for him. Emma Lou wasn't paying any attention to him; she was giving all of her attention to the nest problem. She finally came up with an idea.

"If we moved that little cabinet over by Runt's box, that would fix it. Then she couldn't see the couple under the stove and they couldn't see her. You know, I almost believe it's the faces she makes at them that keeps them stirred up."

Jerome laughed, but he agreed. He studied the string and the button which controlled the door of the cabinet. "I'll have to make a change in the wires to the cabinet."

"I'll help," Emma Lou offered.

Jerome sighed. He would just as soon have put the

job off a day or two, but he knew that once Emma Lou got an idea it had to be worked out at once. He got his tools and started to work. Emma Lou stayed with him until he was well under way, then she wandered off on a mission of her own.

CHAPTER EIGHT

THE MORE Donald thought about his plan to get even with Emma Lou, the better he liked it. He had only a vague knowledge of the game laws, but he knew about the case which had given him his idea. He waited until Emma Lou and Jerome had the fawn well tamed, then he called the game department at Santa Cruz.

As a result of that call Jerome had a visitor one morning. Emma Lou had arrived earlier and had just finished feeding Monarch. She and Jerome were seated on the doorstone in the sun when the visitor arrived.

"You the owner here?" the man asked.

"I am," Jerome said.

"That your black-tailed deer out back?"

"It's one we're raising," Jerome said. "When he gets big enough to take care of himself we'll turn him loose."

"I'm Jim Hinkle, a game warden from Santa Cruz,"

the visitor said. "I suppose you are Jerome Kildee?" He glanced at a small notebook he had taken from his pocket.

"Yes," Jerome said. He was beginning to smell trouble, and so was Emma Lou. She had been brought up to distrust and dislike all game wardens. The Eppys were usually at odds with the local wardens. The Eppy men had a strong feeling they should be allowed to hunt if they wanted to and needed the meat. She jumped to her feet.

"We wouldn't kill Monarch," she said defiantly.

"Probably not, but you are breaking the law. I'm turning the deer loose, and I'll have to file charges against you, Mr. Kildee." He looked down at Emma Lou when he said it. "I guess you had no part in it."

"I did too," Emma Lou said. "I brought the fawn here and asked Jerome to take care of it."

"In that case you are in this too." Mr. Hinkle frowned.

Jerome got to his feet. "Now, officer," he said. "That's my pen and this is my place. I'm the one who's keeping the deer penned up."

"A lion killed his mother, and he'd be dead now if we hadn't taken him in." Emma Lou's eyes were beginning to snap. This man was acting just like a game warden.

Mr. Hinkle smiled at her. "A lion? You wouldn't kid me, miss?" The smile spread into a big grin.

"I can show you the tracks, smarty," Emma Lou said. "I saw him kill her—at least I heard it—and then saw him tearing at her." She stuck her chin out. "Now what do you think of that?"

"I'd say you were seeing things," the warden answered. He turned to Jerome. "If you want to stand trial for this you can have your say in court, but you have been holding a wild deer here in a pen, and that is a violation of the law."

"I'll say it is," Donald's voice broke in. He stepped out from behind the cabin, a big grin on his face. The warden looked at him sharply and knew at once that here was the person who had tipped him off. He figured, too, that there must be bad blood here. That was the way he got most of his tips.

Emma Lou whirled around. "You!" she said from between her teeth. She doubled up her fists and took a step toward Donald. "You dirty tattletale, I'll fix you."

She would have been at Donald if Hinkle had not caught her by the arm. "Easy, now," he said gruffly.

"No use making a fuss, Emma Lou," Jerome said. "I guess I broke the law."

Donald hadn't backed away from Emma Lou. He

spoke as though he had authority. "I guess you can take them in and lock them up, officer."

Jim Hinkle loosed his grip on Emma Lou's arm. "I'm taking nobody in," he snapped. "Mr. Kildee can come in and answer the charge. I reckon he'll have to pay a fine." He paused because Jerome was trying to keep

Emma Lou from flying at Donald. "If your daughter can show me those lion tracks and some evidence of a lion kill, I might forget the whole affair."

Jerome blushed. "She's not my daughter; she's Emma Lou Eppy," he said.

"Oh," Mr. Hinkle said. "One of the nine Eppys?"

"I am," Emma Lou said defiantly.

"Well, now, mebby you did see a lion. If anyone could spot a lion it would be an Eppy." He smiled at Emma Lou.

"I'll show you," she said.

"Lion!" Donald scoffed. "There isn't a lion nearer than Fleishacker's Zoo in the city."

"If I show you lion tracks and some bones and hide where the doe was killed, can we keep Monarch until it's safe for him to leave?" Emma Lou asked. She knew she was gaining an advantage.

"You can't keep him locked up, but if I see even one lion track, and a show that there was a kill, it won't go hard with Mr. Kildee. Could be you've saved a nice buck for some legal hunter." Jim Hinkle wasn't convinced. He figured she would show him bobcat tracks. But this was lion country, and a killer might have drifted in. There hadn't been a cougar reported in more than five years, but it could happen.

Donald wasn't pleased over the way things were going. He laughed. "This is funny," he said. "I suppose she saw a couple of tigers too." No one paid any attention to him.

"Come along," Emma Lou said. She started off across the meadow.

Jim Hinkle and Jerome followed her. Donald hesitated. He was licked and knew it, but he was curious and he hadn't liked being branded a tattletale. There wouldn't be any lion tracks; she had wound the warden around her finger. When Emma Lou reached the edge of the woods she turned around to wait for the men. Donald came up with them. Emma Lou looked him over.

"After I show him the lion tracks and the carcass, I'm going to beat the stuffing out of you."

Donald glared at her. He decided that if there was even one lion track he'd head for home on the double. If he didn't, he'd be in a tight spot. If he fought with her, he'd never live it down, even though he could handle her easily.

Emma Lou led them down the trail. She kept going until she had passed the fern dell, then she left the trail and led them out into the little meadow where the doe had been killed. When she pointed into a clump of dry grass the warden bent forward. There wasn't much left of the doe, just some strips of hide and a few bones; the coyotes and foxes had feasted upon the carcass. Jim Hinkle sat down and studied the remains and the ground. Several times he glanced toward the woods and nodded his head. Getting to his feet, he walked toward the woods.

They watched him as he circled back and forth along the edge of the woods. Emma Lou was ready to take him to a spring and show him some real pad marks, but he seemed to think he would find some near the edge of the woods. Several times he bent down and examined the ground, then he went into the woods. When he came out of the woods he walked across the meadow and faced Emma Lou.

"You are dead right, miss; there was a lion here, and he killed that doe."

Emma Lou shot a triumphant look at Donald. He had stayed well back near the edge of the meadow. Now he turned and headed for the trail. Emma Lou cupped her hands to her mouth and sent a high, rebel yell after him. That yell had been an invention of Job Eppy's father, and it had been copied by a whole company of Stonewall Jackson's men. Job sometimes warmed it up of a morning just to keep it from being forgotten. It made Donald halt in the middle of a blackberry thicket. He stared at Emma Lou. Admiration showed on his face. It was the darnedest yell he had ever heard.

Jim Hinkle stared at Emma Lou, and Jerome's mouth dropped open. The yell had sent chills up Jerome's spine. Hinkle started to grin. "Where'd you learn that trick?" he asked.

"That's the Eppy rebel yell," Emma Lou said, then she blushed because she wasn't supposed to give the yell. Job would have skinned her if he had been there to hear her.

"We'll open that gate," Hinkle said. "If the deer sticks around you can feed it, but the gate has to be open."

Emma Lou smiled up at him. Now that she had saved the day she felt sort of silly. If she hadn't been so mad she never would have threatened to lick Donald, and she wouldn't have cut loose with that awful yell. "Thanks," she said. "I'll feed Monarch and look out for him until he's able to take care of himself."

"With a lion loose he'll need some protection," Hinkle agreed.

"If that lion shows up Ben will get him," Emma Lou said.

Hinkle considered this. "I believe I'll leave him to Ben and your brothers," he said. "I can hardly get a state hunter in here just now."

"Ben will get him," Emma Lou said. She knew her brothers wouldn't want a state hunter in the woods.

"I'll fix it so there won't be any charges, unless that boy makes a fuss, or his old man," Hinkle said.

"I'll take care of him," Emma Lou said.

Jerome broke in quickly. He was afraid Emma Lou was going to tell the officer she would start packing Ben's rifle again. He had an idea the officer wouldn't like that at all.

"It's about dinnertime. You can stay and have a bite with us," he said.

"I'll do just that," Hinkle said. He was glad to be invited. Otherwise he would have to go without eating.

When they reached the house Jim Hinkle was much impressed with Jerome's cabin. He approved of the raccoons, but he dropped a hint of warning about the future.

"You'll have hundreds of 'em, unless you can think of something," he said.

The raccoons were not afraid of Jim Hinkle. As soon as Jerome started popping drawers open they roused themselves from sleep and crowded around. Perhaps they recognized in him a friend and protector. Emma Lou was sorry he wasn't staying until evening so she could show off her skunk tricks. There was little use in trying to get the skunks out from under the house in the middle of the day. He promised to come back later, and he meant it.

The idea of a man having nine wild raccoons and seven skunks living with him appealed to Jim Hinkle. Most of the folks he met shot any wild animal they saw. He knew a hunt club where the owners would have paid Jerome well for his raccoons, just to have them for their hounds to chase, but he didn't mention it. He was sure the idea would have angered Jerome. He knew it would make Emma Lou angry.

Jerome fixed a good dinner which they shared with the raccoons. Jim Hinkle was amused, and amazed at Jerome's inventions. He tried them all and said Jerome should get them patented. He stood for a long time admiring the statue of Old Grouch.

"You did that?" he asked.

"Yes," Jerome said, and felt a warm glow of pride swell inside him.

"It's the best statue I ever saw," Jim Hinkle said.

"It's mine," Emma Lou explained. "Jerome gave it to me, but it looks so swell on his fireplace that I've left it there."

"Sure is the real thing." Jim Hinkle nodded his head. "And the fireplace is something to look at."

Jerome was fast learning that making things people liked and admired was well worth while. He'd have to do a few more pieces. The feeling was so strong that he said:

"I'll do one for you, if you'd like one."

Jim Hinkle hesitated. His salary did not allow him to buy expensive things. "Cost a lot, don't they?" he asked.

"I don't sell them," Jerome said. "I'd give it to you."

"That's mighty nice of you," Jim Hinkle said, and a big smile spread over his face. "You could do about anything, I guess. You do other things besides raccoons?"

Jerome thought of the hundreds of lambs and cherubs and angels he had cut out of marble, but he didn't think Jim Hinkle would be interested in a lamb lying down, or an angel. He said cautiously, "I guess I could cut something else."

"I got a scotty dog, a real little dinger," Jim Hinkle said hopefully.

"I might be able to do him," Jerome said.

"The way you caught the look on that raccoon's face is something. Scotty has a way of cocking his head at you. I'll bet a dollar you could catch it."

Emma Lou had begun to frown. She didn't think the raccoons and the skunks would welcome a scotty dog, not the sort Jim Hinkle was talking about. But Jerome would have to see the dog and know the way he looked.

"If you had a picture of him cocking his head that way——" she began. "I'll have to show you the headstone he made for the lovely lady."

Jerome had started to say he'd have to have the scotty dog up for a while. When Emma Lou suggested a picture he caught on.

Jim Hinkle turned to Emma Lou. "A headstone? Somebody from up here? I've known these hill folks for a long time. Guess I probably knew her."

"She was a raccoon that Cabot kid's dog killed," Emma Lou explained.

"Oh," Jim Hinkle said. "His dog been running loose?" There was a glint in his eyes when he said it.

"He has, and Cabot sicks him onto everything," Emma Lou explained.

"Well, well." Jim Hinkle grinned. He had a hunch he could make sure the Cabots did not press charges against his friends. "I'll just stop at the Cabot place on the way out."

Jerome was squirming uncomfortably. Emma Lou winked at him. Jerome felt he ought to keep the record straight.

"He hasn't let the dog come up here lately," he said.

"It's a big Doberman," Emma Lou hastened to explain. She didn't want Jerome to spoil everything by sticking up for Donald. "But it hasn't sand enough to kill anything unless they run away. It chews up cats and possums and chases deer."

"Chases deer? Well, well." Jim Hinkle frowned deeply and repeated, "Well, well."

"Papa put the run on that dog." Emma Lou was talking fast to keep Jerome from getting in a word.

"Your father?"

"No, the little spotted skunk." Emma Lou grinned.

Jim Hinkle laughed. "Those little stinkers don't come uncorked often, but when they do, they're sure real skunks." He turned to have one last look at Old Grouch on the mantel. "I'll have to get going or I won't get home until late. I'll send up a few good snapshots of Scotty. I'd send him up, but he's a tough little mutt, and Papa might not take to him." He turned and held out his hand to Jerome. "And I'm sure coming back, myself."

They shook hands, with Emma Lou beaming upon them. She had forgotten entirely that Jim Hinkle was a game warden. She liked him. After he had left she sat down at the table and chuckled to herself.

"I hope he takes that dog in with him, and Donald too," she said.

Jerome was looking out through the door. He shook his head. "We're in for trouble," he said. What he meant was that he was in for trouble.

"Trouble?" Emma Lou asked. "Why, we got the best of Cabot, and we got everything fixed for Monarch."

"Sure as I open that gate that deer will be right in the cabin," Jerome said sadly.

Emma Lou realized that Jerome was right. She knew that Monarch had pestered Jerome before they built the pen. He would be ten times as bad now because he was growing like a weed. He wasn't wobbly on his legs any more, and he had developed a playful habit of butting things, including people who turned their backs to him.

"You can make a gate to fit like a screen door," she suggested.

Jerome nodded. He had been thinking about a gate. "Be the only way to keep him out," he agreed.

He set to work making a gate, and he left Monarch penned up until he had the gate hung on its hinges. The gate swung out but could not be pushed inward. It had a spring on it to keep it shut. Emma Lou was sure it would work. Jerome didn't say anything. He decided he'd wait and see if it did work.

They went out and propped the corral gate open. Monarch came bounding out. He bounced around the yard, then started muzzling Emma Lou and Jerome. They retreated into the cabin. He stood with his head over the gate, his big ears propped forward, his tail jerking excitedly. Jerome looked at him. He had a feeling he was going to be more or less of a prisoner in his own house. But after a while Monarch wandered off to explore a world he had seen very little of in his short life. He did not go far, but he examined everything. When he felt tired he returned to his shed and lay down.

Jerome sat outside and smoked. He could hear Emma Lou singing as she went down the trail on her way home. He knew he should not have felt guilty about Donald, but he did. Donald deserved what he had got, but Jerome had a sneaking liking for the boy. He got to wondering if it wasn't just a way every man feels when a woman starts picking on another man, a sort of instinct to stick together. He finally told himself that he wouldn't be bothered with Donald any more. The boy would stay away from his woods from now on.

CHAPTER NINE

RAIN SLOSHED off the eaves and poured down on the white stones at the corners of the house like water tumbling over a cliff. The grass in the meadow was green. Jerome sat at his window drinking coffee. At first the rains were always welcome because they broke a three months' drought during which time not a drop of rain fell. During the dry season every plant dried up except the desert perennials, which had learned to get along with very little moisture. Jerome listened to the rain on the roof. He sighed deeply. If only there would be some thunder, just one earth-shaking clap, or one ragged flash of lightning. He remembered how wild and noisy the rainstorms had been back home. Out here the rain just came down in a steady beating torrent which lasted for days.

Here it was going on Christmas and everything was lush and green and wet. It was hard to imagine the jingle of sleigh bells, or to recall the picture of fields piled high with snow, of naked trees lifting bare branches to a gray sky. It was hard to generate any Christmas spirit. But he did have it, and it was the first time he had ever felt it since he was a boy at home.

Right now he was thinking of a Christmas gift. He wanted to make it a nice one. He wanted to buy Emma Lou a real gift, one she would like, something she wanted. He had hinted and pried for a long time, trying to find out what would please her most.

When school started in the fall she had not been able to visit with him so much. She had chores to do: the cows to milk morning and night, the chickens and the pigs to feed. And she had two miles to walk to school.

He gathered that the only thing she really liked about school was that it gave her a chance at Donald Roger Cabot five days a week. Jerome was glad he wasn't the teacher. And he didn't see just how a one-room school could hold both of them. Emma Lou kept him up to date on the feud. He was glad she had given up the idea of shooting Donald. She had worked out other ways of irritating him. He was not a foe to avoid battle, nor were his tactics always above reproach.

Donald had surprised his parents by insisting upon attending the little one-room school below his home. The teacher soon decided it was not a desire for democracy which made him choose to attend a country school. She suspected it was because it gave him a chance to fight with Emma Lou Eppy.

But the Cabot-Eppy battle did not keep Emma Lou away from Jerome's house. Her main interests in life were still the raccoons and the skunks and the advancement of Monarch. True, her thoughts were often diverted because it took some heavy thinking to keep ahead of Donald, but she gave Jerome and his friends all of the time she could spare.

Jerome's household had settled down for the winter. The raccoons were really housekeeping now. Each pair had a nice nest which was jealously guarded. Old Grouch had a cushion by the fireplace. He remained true to the memory of the lovely lady, so he did not need a box. The little skunks had all grown up, but they still lived under the house with Papa and Mama. They were a very happy family and came in for a frolic every night.

Monarch had set off to see the world, at least that part of it guarded by the Pacific fog banks. He roamed the lush meadows and spent many hours in the green twilight of the big woods. He was a spike buck now, and his place in the pattern of things was secure. His visits to the cabin became fewer as the rainy season advanced. At last he stopped coming entirely, though he still stayed on Jerome's mountain, and Emma Lou was able to keep track of him.

Jerome poured himself another cup of coffee. He could buy her a wrist watch. But Emma Lou would probably break it the first time she climbed a tree. She never wore any jewelry. Jerome pondered and finally gave it up. He'd have to do some more hinting.

Without Emma Lou around, Jerome was lazy. He kept putting off doing things. He was supposed to have everything ready for a Christmas party, and he should put the finishing touches on Jim Hinkle's statue of Scotty. The little statue was turning out rather well, and he was sure Hinkle would like it. He could put off finishing the statue, but he couldn't put off getting things ready for the party. One thing about having met Emma Lou was that his easy way of living was no more. She was always thinking of things he could do and seeing that he did them. This party had been his idea, but once he had mentioned it, Emma Lou had helped plan it.

It could not be held on Christmas Eve because she had to go to a party at the school, where the community was having a tree, but it was to be a Christmas party for Jerome and for the raccoons and the little spotted skunks. Emma Lou let Jerome believe the party was mostly for the raccoons and the little skunks, but it was really for him. She had a present for him, and Cilly was making a cake.

Jerome got to his feet. He opened the door and sniffed the wet woodsy smell in the air. He had to get boughs and a tree. Getting into his slicker, he put on his boots and rain hat. He grinned as he trudged through the rain. He had an idea the raccoons would eat the toyon berries off the branches he brought in, and he had an idea they might do things to the tree decorations Emma Lou was bringing up with her.

Emma Lou was at the house when he got back, loaded down with toyon branches and redwood boughs. She had gathered an armload of pine and fir boughs for around the fireplace. Jerome was careful to pile the toyon branches on the table. Big clusters of red berries gave the toyon limbs a Christmasy look. Emma Lou had put the ornaments and the candles on the mantel. The rush of fragrance from the boughs had roused the raccoons. They were prowling about, sniffing and chattering excitedly.

"See how quickly they catch the Christmas spirit," Emma Lou said.

Jerome grinned. "They know something is up."

"The first job is to get the tree on a stand," Emma Lou said.

"I have that all fixed," Jerome answered. He had

given the tree base some thought and had decided to make it solid. One or all of the raccoons might decide to climb the tree. He set the tree into the base he had made and nailed it fast. Emma Lou started stringing decorations. When she got out the silver balls to hang on the tips of the branches the raccoons really got interested. Runt dashed around and around the tree. Her burly husband sat under a limb, staring up at a silver ball. The bright trinkets had the raccoons in a real tizzy. After a bit they all sat down and just stared up at the pretty things.

"They love it," she said.

Old Grouch was the only one not affected by the tree. He looked it over, grunted a couple of times, then returned to his cushion, where he curled up and went to sleep.

"He's the only one who doesn't believe in Santa Claus," Emma Lou said.

"We better leave the candles off until just before we light them," Jerome suggested.

"They'll eat them," Emma Lou said. "But the candles won't hurt them. When I was little I ate them."

With the tree decorated, they gave their attention to the toyon berry branches. They tacked them high on the wall, leaving the redwood and pine boughs lower down. Emma Lou was perched on a chair, putting a branch into place. Suddenly she let out a yelp. Jerome turned around. His mouth was full of tacks, so all he could do was sputter. Runt had climbed the tree. She was seated on a branch, and she had a silver ball in her paws. She was trying to poke a slim claw into the hole where the clip had been. She was sure there must be something wonderful inside the shiny ball.

Emma Lou hopped off the chair. Runt saw her coming and knew she was after the silver ball. She slid out of the tree and scooted for the door, clutching her prize. Tinfoil streamed out behind her and waved from her tail. Emma Lou halted and placed her hands on her hips. Jerome emptied the tacks out of his mouth.

"That solves a problem," she said.

"I don't know." Jerome was eying a raccoon who had slipped around behind the tree.

"I couldn't think of anything to give them as presents except something to eat. They can have the ornaments." She grinned at Jerome.

"Looks like they are going to get them anyway," Jerome said.

Within an hour there wasn't an ornament on the tree. They were all in the nests of the raccoons. Runt came in dripping wet, but she had her ornament. She dashed to her nest and hid it under the cotton bedding.

Emma Lou had to rush home. "I'll be up about seven to help put on the candles and light them."

Jerome started to call her back when she turned toward the door. Her present would be late because he had not found out what she wanted. "I'll fix something to eat," he said.

"We'll be up early," she said. "I'll get here ahead of

the others." She ducked out into the rain before Jerome could get any hints.

Jerome shook his head. He was glad the Eppy family was coming for the party, but he wasn't sure they could all get inside his house. It seemed a little odd to him that they'd want to come. He had never visited with them. He could not know how much curiosity Emma Lou had aroused by her talk of things that went on at Jerome's house. Only a great curiosity would have got all of the Eppys out on a rainy night. Ben had added his report of what went on in Jerome's house, and that had clinched the matter. When Emma Lou suggested a party they were all eager to go.

Jerome made a decision while he sat looking at the tree. He took out his billfold and removed a ten-dollar bill. He put it into an envelope and wrote Emma Lou's name on it and a big MERRY CHRISTMAS. He put it up on the base of the Old Grouch statue, where she would be sure to see it. Then he busied himself getting things ready for his guests.

CHAPTER TEN

JEROME had a pile of sandwiches made and the water for the coffee was boiling. He had candy and nuts and oranges in a bowl on the table. While he worked at the stove he had to keep one eye on the table. The raccoons were sitting around it, looking up at the heaping bowl of sweets. The seven little skunks had come in shortly after dark. They seemed to know that this was a special occasion. They were busy under the bed looking for mice. There were no mice left now. The seven hunters had proved too much for even the old ones. But there was still a mousy smell which kept the hunters poking about.

Jerome had just finished counting the sandwiches. He thought three apiece would be enough, but he had made four extras. He put down the carving knife and turned toward the door. It opened and a gust of wet wind blew in. Emma Lou came in with the gust, red-cheeked and sparkling with rain. Cilly was close behind her. Then Job came in, ducking off his dripping hat, and mopping the rain from his beard.

"Merry Christmas," Emma Lou shouted. "I couldn't get away early."

Jerome grinned at them. One after another, the six Eppy boys entered the room, ducking their heads as they always did when they walked through an ordinary doorway. They stood grinning at Jerome, their eyes taking in his odd house. They filled the cabin, and they formed such tight ranks that the startled raccoons could not escape. They did the next best thing; they dashed for their nests and tumbled into them.

"Find places to sit down," Jerome said. "My house is a bit small."

Each of the boys carried a basket. Cilly was so busy looking around the room that she hadn't told the boys what to do with them, so they held the baskets and their dripping hats.

"My, it's nice," Cilly said.

"We came along on account of Emma Lou. She's been at us for a week," Job said.

"Glad you came," Jerome said. "It's Emma Lou's party."

"Had to see them trick skunks," Amby said. He was

looking around for a place to set his basket. It seemed to be very heavy.

Emma Lou and Cilly took over at once. The baskets were set on the floor near the stove. They got the Eppy men and Jerome seated on the bed, the chairs, and the hearth. Jerome caught himself stealing glances at the husky Eppys. They were broad-shouldered as well as tall, and their shocks of hair ranged from blond to a red as dark as Emma Lou's. Amby and Ben were seated on the hearth. Ben nudged Amby and nodded toward the bed. Seven pairs of bright little eyes were peering out at them.

"The skunks," Ben said.

"Cute little critters." Amby made a clucking sound with his tongue, which was answered by a chorus of churrs from under the bed.

"I still don't believe they do tricks," Dave said as he began filling his pipe.

Dave started something by getting out his pipe. Job looked at Jerome, and when Jerome got out his pipe and passed his tobacco jar to Dave they all got out pipes, except Ben, who looked at Job sourly. Job grinned at him.

"Bein' this is Christmas, and that I've been a-smellin' tobacco on you fer a month, you kin smoke," Job said.

Ben grinned sheepishly. He dug into his pocket and

brought out a new pipe. It was a very small pipe. Amby laughed when he saw it. "Pewee stuff," he jeered.

They lighted up, and soon Cilly had to open the door to let the smoke out of the room. She and Emma Lou were taking pies and cakes, cookies, cold meat, and jars of fruit and preserves from the baskets. Jerome's eyes bugged out as they stacked the table high with things to eat. They had brought along enough food to feed him and his animals a month. He stole a glance at the platter of sandwiches he had made. The pile looked puny beside the huge haunch of roast sitting beside it. Amby's basket contained three gallon jugs of cider.

The raccoons could not keep their heads down inside their boxes, with so many good smells filling the room. The noses of the little skunks, poked out from under Jerome's spread, twitched eagerly. The raccoons and the skunks would have enjoyed the smells a lot more if the air had not been well filled with pipe smoke.

When Cilly and Emma Lou had everything set out Emma Lou lighted the fire in the fireplace. Jerome had left that for her because she liked to start the fire roaring. Ben and Amby had stood up. They were admiring the statue of Old Grouch.

"Perfect picture of an old raccoon," Amby said.

"Looks just like the tough old customer that licked Ma Grady," Ben said.

Emma Lou stood up. "It is the same old raccoon. Right now he's asleep under the bed." Then she saw the envelope. "Is it for me?" she asked.

"It's for you," Jerome said.

Emma Lou opened the envelope. "Oh," she said. "It's too much." She had never had ten dollars of her own in her whole life.

Jerome grinned at her. "Thought you'd know best what you want."

"You can get some nice print dresses," Cilly said. "And wear them," she added.

"I'm going to get a pair of boots," Emma Lou said.

"When do we eat?" Enoch asked. They were the first words he had spoken since entering the house.

"I thought we'd have some fun first," Emma Lou said.

"Rather eat first," Amby said. "That's fun."

"All right, but you might forget your stomach for one night." Emma Lou made a face at her brother.

The seven Eppys tucked away their pipes. They crowded around the table. Jerome joined them, but he didn't shove right in. There was a lot of pushing and laughing and joking as the men filled their plates. Jerome decided there might not be too much food after all. By the time they had filled their plates the haunch of meat had shrunken to a small roast, his sandwiches were all gone, and one cake had vanished.

"While you're eating I'll have the skunks do their trick," Emma Lou said. "If we wait they'll beg so much stuff they won't act for me."

To keep the raccoons out of the act, she set a platter of meat scraps and cake on the floor near the stove. They scurried to it and gathered around, keeping one eye on the Eppys while they ate. The little skunks were getting over their shyness toward the giants who had come into their house. It was their nature not to be really afraid of any animal. The good smells were so strong they just could not stay hidden. Papa stepped out from under the bed and sat up. Emma Lou had set out the seven cylinders of bay wood. She tapped on one of them with a pencil. Mama trotted out from under the bed. Emma Lou tapped some more, and the five youngsters scampered out. They ran to the cylinders and perched on them and draped their paws over their furry stomachs. Mama and Papa joined them. As Emma Lou moved the pencil back and forth their heads moved back and forth in unison. When she lowered the pencil to the floor they all bowed. Then she gave each of them a piece of roast. Instantly they hopped off their perches and dashed under the bed.

"I'll be gol-danged," Ben said, and slapped his leg.

Job's hearty laugh filled the cabin. The boys joined him. The burst of laughter sent the seven skunks flying

for the door. Cilly had closed the big door, so they zipped out through the little door. Mama barely made it ahead of Runt's burly husband, who knocked Runt over in his dash to get outside. Runt was badly trampled in the stampede of the raccoons, but she managed to get outside close on the heels of the last raccoon. Old Grouch came out from under the bed and stood staring at the invaders. He marched to the door, sniffing and growling. The Eppys roared with laughter. When they had quieted down Job said:

"Reckon we scared 'em away. Now we won't see the rest of the show."

"The raccoons will be back," Emma Lou said. "The little skunks will probably go hunting in the rain. They'd rather catch their own food, anyway."

The skunks did not come back, but the raccoons returned. They stuffed themselves and sat in their boxes, grunting happily, while Jerome and Emma Lou put the candles on the tree and lighted them. The three jugs of cider went dry, and the cakes and cookies vanished. All that was left of the stacks of food was the bare bone on the roast platter. Job finally pulled out a big silver watch and looked at it. He turned to Cilly. "Fifteen to nine, Cilly," he said.

All of the Eppys stood up. They put their plates and cups and dishes into the baskets, and the boys picked them up. They grinned at Jerome. They liked his cabin. They liked him, but they weren't much on talking, so they didn't tell him that they had had a good time. Cilly made up for them. She said:

"It has been a nice party. You'll have to come down and have dinner with us someday."

They all filed out, leaving Emma Lou for a final word with Jerome. She seemed a bit worried. "Did you like it, honest?" She fished a holly-wrapped box from her pocket. "Here's a Christmas present I made for you." She shoved it into his hands, then ducked out fast.

Jerome stood in the doorway, watching her dash away

into the rainy night after the family. Flashlights bobbed as the Eppys headed down the trail toward home. Jerome smiled happily. Not many neighbors would walk a mile up a wet trail with the night as black as the inside of a hat just to visit with a man who had never even stopped at their house for a word. And to pack all that food up with them! Emma Lou certainly had a way of getting what she wanted done.

Outside the wind began moaning around the eaves. It drove the rain against the window in sheets. Jerome began to smile. It was good to hear the wind and to listen to the slashing rain after weeks of silent dripping. He got up and put two more logs on the fire, then he snuffed the candles on the tree. Settling himself before the fire, he lighted his pipe.

In a very short time Jerome had his storm. It roared in from the Pacific, tearing at the limbs of his giant tree. Jerome wasn't worried. There never had been a storm which could move the great tree. Then the tree began to sway just a little, moving back and forth. He felt the floor move, and a board buckled and cracked. He caught himself wishing the wind would let up a little. He had read a pamphlet on redwoods, and the writer had said that the only power able to fell a giant redwood, aside from the axes and saws of lumbermen, was wind. Sometimes hurricanes blew the giants down. Jerome's tree was more than two hundred feet high. At a hundred feet from the ground it was eighteen feet in circumference. Such a giant was worthy of a hurricane's strength; it was a challenge. The storm tore at the tree, and the tree moved. The roof began to leak where he had joined it to the tree.

Sparks and soot and bits of burning wood sucked up the chimney as the wind pulled the air out of the house, taking even the heat up the chimney. Jerome sat by the fire and watched the bark wall of his house. If the tree fell it would smash his house. He was sure of this because of the direction of the wind. It would smash him too. He ought to leave and make his way down to the Eppy place. Jerome listened to the great tree. It was not moaning; it was roaring at the storm in a lusty voice. He leaned back. The giant had been defying storms for a thousand, possibly two thousand, years. He started to laugh. He wouldn't desert the giant. But he would go to bed to keep warm.

He got ready for bed, but he didn't crawl in between the blankets. He sat huddled before the fire and listened to the battle of the giants. The raccoons were unworried. They were stuffed with food, and this was their playtime. They had poked their noses through the little door and had decided the night was too rough to venture out into the woods. Jerome heard the little skunks come scurrying to their nest under the floor. The night was too bad outside for them. They chased about under the floor for a while, then came into the cabin. The storm seemed to make them wild. It had the same effect on the raccoons. The skunks bluffed the raccoons and chased them, but they could not drive the raccoons out into the storm. Not one of his friends seemed in the least worried about the big tree. Watching them, Jerome felt better, but he didn't feel secure enough to go to bed. He sat close to the fire and waited.

A powerful gust of wind tore at the tree. The tree gave more than before and opened the gap between the roof and the tree to a wide crack. Water poured in. Jerome got to his feet and began moving things. One of the raccoons' boxes had been hit by a bucket of water. The two raccoons were in it. They climbed out, shaking themselves and scolding. They scolded Jerome and not the storm. They were so peeved at him that Jerome had to laugh. He emptied the water out of the box and set it in a dry spot. They joined the other raccoons playing tag by the door.

Jerome piled more wood on the fire and sat close to it. If the tree fell there was nothing he could do, not as long as he stayed and sat waiting to be smashed.

The big tree did not fall. It settled back into position, and the roof crack closed as the soft bark squeezed tight against the boards. The river of water stopped running across the floor. Jerome listened and decided the wind was slackening. But he stayed up for another hour. By that time the wind had lost its fury, and the big tree did not move at all. Jerome got into bed. He hoped the Eppys had reached home before the storm broke. But he did not worry much about them. It would take a powerful wind to blow those giants off a trail. Emma Lou and Cilly would be well protected, he was sure of that

CHAPTER ELEVEN

THE RAINS had slacked off. The steady weeping of the skies had changed to showers with sunshine in between, and fog rolling up the deep valleys at night. The fog seldom reached as high up the mountain as Jerome's house. It was March weather, summer-warm, but winter-green, a fine time to wander in the woods because wild flowers were blooming in solid fields, with acres of golden poppies nodding to every breeze.

But Jerome was not enjoying the beautiful weather. He was worn out; his eyes were red, and his nerves jumpy. All week long the stork had been visiting his house. And that worthy bird had been liberal. Now that the visits were over he found himself host to exactly twenty-five raccoons, four broods nestling in four boxes, and guarded by four watchful mothers. Runt had six babies, and her husky mate was very proud, though not in high favor. He was forced to sleep on the floor just outside the box. The smallest family was in the nest under the stove. That pair had only two young ones.

Jerome tried hard not to give the future a thought. And for a few days he did not worry because he slept most of the time. But he had duties to perform and could not sleep all of the time. It was impossible to sleep when the raccoons got hungry. There was one small ray of comfort. The fathers had taken to making long trips into the woods. They were not welcome in the nests and

would not be for a while. Jerome knew it was only temporary relief, but it helped a little.

He had another thing to make him uneasy. Papa and Mama had shooed their children off into the woods some weeks back. Jerome had a feeling the five youngsters would locate five mates and return. The possibility was that he would wake up some morning and find himself godfather to some thirty little spotted skunks. Thirty skunks, twenty-five raccoons. When he couldn't drop off to sleep he counted skunks, and not sheep.

The raccoon families had arrived during the week. Jerome had slept through Friday night and late Saturday morning. He had been up less than an hour and was sipping coffee at his window when Emma Lou arrived. The raccoon mothers had been fed and were back in their boxes. Old Grouch was the only male in the house. He acted a bit uncertain. Jerome thought he swaggered a bit. The fathers had finally given up sleeping on the hard floor and were off in the woods, where they could have comfortable beds. The raccoon feeding problem had been solved by the discovery that the raccoons liked canned corn about as much as bears like honey. He had three cases of canned corn stacked in a corner. He grinned at Emma Lou as she appeared in the doorway. He was eager to tell her the news. Now that he had caught up on his sleep the outlook did not seem so gloomy. But Emma Lou had news and told hers first.

"I just peeked under the house," she announced. Jerome saw she was carrying a small flashlight. "Some of the children have come home married. I'm not sure, but I think there're five nests under there, anyway four." She tossed her hat on the floor. "Isn't it wonderful!"

"It is," Jerome agreed. "And you might take a peek into the raccoon boxes."

"Oh!" She turned quickly toward Runt's box. "Have they all arrived?"

"All," Jerome said.

Emma Lou bent over Runt's box. Runt looked up at her proudly. When Emma Lou lifted her out of the box she churred happily. "Six babies!" Emma Lou squealed with delight. "Runt, you're wonderful."

She dropped Runt back into the box and tiptoed around, peeping into each nest. When she came back to the table she had a dreamy look on her face. She sat down and smiled at Jerome. "Sixteen babies," she said softly.

"Twenty-five raccoons," Jerome said. "By next March there'll be one hundred and twenty-five." He paused. "The March after that there'll be six hundred and twenty-five."

Emma Lou considered this for a time. Finally she laughed. "I'll think of something."

"I could add another story and live upstairs," Jerome said.

Emma Lou giggled. "Every year you could add another story and move up a little higher." They both laughed at the idea of a house growing to be two hundred feet high.

"I'd do it if they'd let me keep the ground-floor room," Jerome said.

"Could you afford to do it and feed them, too?" Emma Lou asked. The idea really appealed to her.

"I guess not," Jerome said. "Anyway, we'd have to figure out something for the skunks."

"It wouldn't be fair to leave them out." Emma Lou sighed. "But it's a grand idea." She got up and walked to the door. "We could build little houses outside, a house for each family."

Jerome remembered how Mrs. Grouch had always returned her brood to the oven. He had taken them out of the oven and scrubbed it with Dutch Cleanser every Saturday afternoon so he could cook his roast. "They'd pack the babies right back into the house," he said.

Emma Lou was really pleased the way things were, but she knew the raccoons would be a bother to Jerome, and there was the future to think about, of course. Jerome was going to live with the raccoons all of the time;

she would only be up on visits. She smiled brightly. "We'll work out something."

"There'll probably be twenty-five or thirty little skunks," Jerome said. "With such a gang around, I doubt if we can help having trouble. Looks like I'll have to do something."

"Thirty would be quite a few skunks along with the raccoons," Emma Lou admitted. "But it would be wonderful having thirty skunks in my act. It hasn't been nearly so good since I've just had Mama and Papa."

Jerome grinned. It would be something, watching her put thirty skunks through the act. "We could handle the skunks if we didn't have a raccoon for every square foot of the floor."

"Could I have an egg and some bacon?" Emma Lou asked. "I can't think when I'm hungry. I was so eager to find out what had happened that I didn't wait for breakfast."

"I'll fix two eggs," Jerome said with a grin. "I think you'll need an extra egg to help solve this one."

"I can fix them," Emma Lou said. "All we've had is venison for a week." She scowled. "And Ben wouldn't tell me anything. He won't tell me a thing now that I've made friends with Jim Hinkle. But he acted funny. I couldn't eat a bite of venison."

Jerome regarded her thoughtfully. Finally he said,

"Has Monarch been around lately?" He had a hunch this would get at the real trouble regarding the venison.

"I did see him, and he knew me." Emma Lou's eyes were snapping now. "But I haven't seen him for a week." She stuck out her chin and stabbed at the sizzling bacon with her fork. "I'll get even with Ben."

"It probably wasn't Monarch," Jerome said soothingly.

"I ought to tell Jim Hinkle." She flipped the pair of eggs and smacked them with the turner. "Ben hasn't any hundred dollars. If he had to stay in jail it would teach him something."

Jerome frowned. "You wouldn't do that to Ben," he said.

"Well, no, but I'll do something to him." She looked down at the four mama raccoons who had gathered around her and were sniffing eagerly. "Could I boil them an egg?"

"Better make it two," Jerome said. "They'd get one eaten before you finished yours and beg your breakfast off you."

She boiled two eggs for the raccoons. After they were chopped and set on the floor she carried her plate to the table and sat down. She had to get her mind off Monarch. She needed to give some thought to Jerome's problems.

Emma Lou stayed for lunch. She did not feel up to facing another meal of venison. But she had work to do and had to leave shortly after lunch. Cilly was having a spell of rheumatism and needed help with the housework. There was also a new calf to be cared for. She couldn't think of any plan to help Jerome, but she felt there would be time enough for that before the young raccoons and the young skunks began getting around.

Jerome did not move from his seat by the window. A long tramp through the woods was what he needed, but he was too weary to move. The sound of a step on his doorstone made him turn his head.

"Hello." Donald grinned as he greeted Jerome.

"Hello," Jerome answered. He was so surprised he forgot to invite the boy inside.

"Thought I'd come up and see how your zoo was coming along," Donald said. "I've been thinking about visiting you for some time."

"Come in," Jerome said, "and have a chair." He tipped the chair forward across the table, dumping Old Grouch onto the floor. Old Grouch bounced up, fluffing his fur and growling. He blinked a couple of times as he saw Donald, then he marched past the boy and out into the yard.

Donald sat down beside the table. Jerome was sure

he wanted something, so he waited. Donald was somewhat embarrassed. Finally he said, "I guess I've been sort of nasty."

Jerome considered this for a minute. He really did not dislike Donald. He should not like him, but there was something about the boy that appealed to him.

"If it wasn't for that redhead I'd like to come up here often." Donald scowled. "If she wasn't a girl I could fix her quick and plenty."

Jerome smiled. "But she is a girl," he said. "And a mighty nice one."

"Ben Eppy's been working for Dad."

Jerome nodded. He was beginning to see that Emma Lou had more than just Monarch to hold against Ben. He had an idea Ben and Donald had been deer hunting, and that perhaps Emma Lou suspected they had bagged Monarch.

"Ben says you have seven skunks, and that they do tricks," Donald said. He had come to the reason for visiting Jerome. He had to see those seven skunks do their tricks.

"I don't rightly know how many skunks I have right now," Jerome said. "At a guess I'd say there were twelve, and that after a bit there'll be thirty or more."

Donald stared at him openmouthed. "Thirty skunks?" It was clear he did not believe it.

"It may work out that way," Jerome said.

"And Ben says you have nine raccoons."

"Twenty-five raccoons," Jerome said.

"Golly, twenty-five raccoons." Donald looked around the room. He saw four bandit faces peeping at him over the edges of four boxes.

"Six young ones in that box." Jerome nodded toward Runt's nest. "Some in each nest."

"What you going to do with them?" Donald was amazed, and he was impressed.

"I don't know," Jerome admitted. "But I'll have to do something or move out."

Donald grinned. He shook his head. "Thirty skunks and twenty-five raccoons. That's sure swell."

Jerome smiled because he had used the same words Emma Lou had used.

"Can you teach the thirty skunks to do tricks?" Donald asked eagerly. "Ben says they do their tricks all together."

"Emma Lou teaches them their tricks," Jerome said.

Donald frowned. "If that redhead can teach them tricks, so can I."

Jerome thought this over. He didn't much like the idea of having them meet in his house. It wouldn't be as bad as a fight between the skunks and the raccoons, but it might be unpleasant. And it would probably be as one-sided as a fight between the skunks and the raccoons. Emma Lou had a decided advantage.

"They won't be big enough to start training for a long time," he said.

Donald got to his feet. "I'll come up once in a while. If you don't mind." He added as he paused in the doorway, "I'll make sure the redhead isn't here. I know how to fix her, but I wouldn't make trouble for you."

"Come up any time she's not here," Jerome said, and meant it.

"And I'll think of something to help you out. I'd like to have what you can't keep up here, but my folks wouldn't let me keep them." He paused just outside the door. "You don't think so many skunks and raccoons will mix very well?" He grinned back at Jerome.

"That's part of the problem," Jerome admitted.

"I'll think of something."

"Between the three of us we ought to think of some solution," Jerome said. "Emma Lou is doing some thinking too."

Donald bristled at once. "We'll see who comes up with an idea that will work," he said.

Jerome grinned as he watched Donald stride down the slope. He was probably asking for trouble in inviting the boy to visit him, but one more trouble wouldn't break his back.

CHAPTER TWELVE

JEROME was as fussed as a mother hen with two broods of chicks. For a week the young raccoons had been getting out of their nests and exploring the house. Every time Jerome took a step he had to look to make sure he didn't step on a young bandit. The skunk families had arrived, and as near as he could make out there would be twenty-seven spotted skunks frisking in and out of his house as soon as the little ones grew big enough to follow their mothers. The father raccoons had returned to help with the raising of their children.

To add to his worries Donald was coming up regularly. He was spending a lot of time on the hill. At first he had been very careful to scout the place before showing himself, but of late he was getting careless. The raccoons fascinated him, and he was impatient for the day when the skunks would all march into the house. It was wearing on the nerves, having him barely miss bumping into

Emma Lou. So far neither of them had come up with any ideas as to what Jerome was going to do about the housing problem.

So far the raccoons and the skunks had got along. The mother and father skunks came up for food, but they always hurried back to their young ones. The little raccoons seemed to understand from the start that they had better not bother the skunks. But there was no telling what would happen when the skunks started bringing their youngsters into the house. The skunks might decide to clean out the raccoons once for all. Trouble could start over anything, a bit of meat, or a scared baby skunk calling for help when a big raccoon popped out from under the bed a few inches away.

One day Donald brought a squirrel cage up from his place. It had a wheel in it for the squirrels to use as a race track. Donald took one end out of the cage so the little skunks could get in and out. The papa and mama skunks soon discovered what the wheel was for and had gay times racing around and around. Sometimes as many as three tried to use the wheel at the same time. This always caused a wild scramble and considerable loud talk. As soon as Donald left, Jerome hid the cage so that Emma Lou would not see it. But the skunks liked it so much that he put it back after she left.

One evening he forgot to hide it, and the next day

Emma Lou saw it. She pounced upon it and called for Jerome.

"Look what I found," she said when Jerome poked his head out of the door. "That Cabot wretch has sneaked up here and is trying to trap our skunks."

Jerome came out and stood blinking at the cage. He knew he wouldn't be able to tell Emma Lou a fib she would believe.

"It's not a trap," he said.

Emma Lou frowned at the cage. She wasn't convinced. Just then a pair of skunks slipped out from under the house. They hopped into the cage and darted to the wheel. Round and round they went in a giddy whirl of flying feet and waving plumes. Emma Lou watched them for a time, then she sat down beside the cage. After a while she started to laugh.

"They love it," she said slowly. Then she looked up at Jerome and saw that he was looking very guilty. "He's been coming up here, hasn't he?"

"Yes."

Emma Lou's eyes followed the little skunk who was still racing inside the wheel. Jerome waited for the blow-up he was sure was coming. After a bit she said:

"I guess he has as much right up here as I do." She got to her feet. "I guess I'll be getting on home."

Jerome wanted to say something, but he couldn't

think of anything. He had expected her to blow up and kick things around; instead she just looked hurt. She acted as though Jerome had ordered her off his mountain. She was gone before he could think of any way to explain matters to her.

An hour later Donald arrived. Jerome was feeling very low. He felt like a traitor. Donald noticed he looked worried. "Don't you worry about a thing," he said. "I'm working on a grand scheme." He grinned broadly. "I'll clear your cabin of every raccoon and every skunk you want to get rid of."

Jerome perked up at once. "I won't sell any of them. Not one goes to a fur farm, or to any hunt club. I'll move out and give them the house before I let any bunch of hunters chase them with dogs."

"Nothing like that," Donald said cheerfully.

"Well, that wasn't what was worrying me," Jerome said. "Why can't you and Emma Lou stop fighting?"

Donald looked at Jerome sharply. "She's found out I'm coming up here?"

"Yes, and she walked out on me. I doubt if she comes back. She thinks I double-crossed her," Jerome said.

"Good riddance," Donald said cheerfully. "But she'll come back."

"She wasn't mad, she just walked away," Jerome said.

"Forget it," Donald advised. "I brought a sack of

roasting ears up for the coons. I read in a book that they go for green corn." He picked up the sack he had set on the doorstone and walked into the house.

Jerome followed him indoors. Donald pulled an ear of corn from the sack. He stripped back the husks and broke off a piece of the ear. A half dozen big and little raccoons had crowded around and were sniffing eagerly.

Runt was the quickest and got the piece of corn ear first.

Being a California raccoon, she knew nothing of the delicious, milky flavor of a roasting ear. Holding the ear in her paws, she nibbled off a kernel and sampled it. Her eyes began to sparkle, and she looked around suspiciously to make sure none of the other raccoons were close enough to snatch the prize from her. Quickly she snipped off the kernels and munched them. Her youngsters crowded around demanding a taste, but she sat up very straight and refused to let them have a kernel. When her big mate ambled over and thrust out his snout, she snapped at him. He backed away and sat down, a gloomy expression coming over his face.

Donald laughed. He began passing out pieces of corn ear. Every raccoon, big and little, got a sample, and they liked it. There was much growling and snapping and pure enjoyment. Jerome forgot his gloom and enjoyed the scene.

Donald passed out the last of the corn. As he poked the husks into the sack he said, "Wish I could stay until the skunks come out, but I have to be home for dinner tonight."

Jerome laughed. He felt pretty good all of a sudden. And it had all hit him like a flash of bright light. "How about having supper with me tomorrow night? I'll need some help. Fact is, I've been fastening the little door to keep the skunk families out. Tomorrow night we'll let them get acquainted with the raccoons."

"Sure," Donald said. "I'll bring along some stuff." He tried to hide his eagerness. It was the first time Jerome had asked him up for a meal or for the evening.

"Don't bring anything. This is to be my party," Jerome said.

Donald knew he had made a slip. "Sure," he said. "Just don't want to sponge." He smiled quickly. "You have a mob to feed anyway."

"I don't mind it a bit," Jerome said. "I can afford to feed you too."

Donald nodded. He knew Jerome wasn't poor, but it was hard to think of him as a man of means because of the way he lived. He got to his feet and picked up his sack. Runt hopped about eagerly. He tossed her some peanuts. There was quite a scramble as the peanuts rolled across the floor. One little fellow got the wadded cellophane bag. He jumped up on the oven door and carefully unwrapped it. Then he thrust a paw into it and was rewarded by finding half of a peanut in one corner.

"I'll be up for dinner," Donald said as he opened the door.

Jerome grinned at him. "I'll be expecting you."

The door closed behind Donald and, Jerome lighted his pipe. He leaned back in his chair and put his feet on the table. He ought to get up and latch the little door. The skunks had started taking their babies for walks. They'd be bringing them into the cabin any evening now. But Old Grouch was still off in the woods. Jerome saw him coming across the meadow. He shoved through the little door. He snapped at one of the young raccoons, then showed his teeth when the mother dashed to her youngster. He ambled over to Jerome's chair and sat down. His fat stomach settled down around his feet like a well-filled sack. He grunted sourly. Jerome blew a cloud of smoke at him.

"It will be worth trying," Jerome said.

Old Grouch growled. He wasn't agreeing with anyone.

"Might work." Jerome puffed deeply.

"May I come in?" a polite voice asked from the door.

Jerome turned his head. Emma Lou was standing there. He had never heard her speak that way, so he had not recognized her voice.

"Sure, come in. You don't have to ask." He smiled at her eagerly.

"I came to get the statue of Old Grouch," Emma Lou said. "I'd like to have it for my room."

"It's yours," Jerome said.

Emma Lou entered. The raccoons closed in around her. She hesitated, then she knelt down. She didn't miss the gnawed cobs Jerome hadn't got around to sweeping up, or the peanut bag one of the little raccoons was playing with, but she didn't say anything. She sat on the floor and gathered as many raccoons into her lap as it would hold.

"I got some news," she said. "Thought you'd like to know."

"You bet I would," Jerome said.

"I saw Monarch today. He was way up on the ridge above the sawmill."

"That's fine," Jerome said. "I'm glad he's safe." He rubbed his chin thoughtfully. Emma Lou had sure taken a long hike, to be up above the sawmill. Four miles at least.

She set the raccoons on the floor and got to her feet. Jerome watched her lift the little statue from the mantel. He smiled at her. "I figure the little skunks may pay me a visit tonight. I haven't had any help, so I've kept the little door latched. We could have a bite and see if they come."

"I have to get home." She was looking at the cobs on the floor.

"How about coming to supper tomorrow night?" Jerome asked. "They're almost sure to visit me tomorrow night."

Emma Lou looked at the statue thoughtfully. Then

she looked at Jerome. "I guess I can come," she said.

"Good. I'll cook up something special."

After Emma Lou had gone he latched the little door. He chuckled to himself as he fixed supper. He heard scratching sounds at the little door, but he didn't open it. He would save that for tomorrow night. After supper he swept up the cobs and cleaned a few small spots with Clorox. He fed Old Grouch and the rest of his tribe. Old Grouch mellowed under the influence of the food and Jerome's attention. They sat before the open fire for quite a while.

The scratching started again, and with it came sounds of gnawing. Jerome got up and fixed a tray of chopped meat and bread crumbs. He set them just outside his door. Many bright eyes twinkled in the reflected light as the skunks crowded around.

"You're all invited for tomorrow night," he said as he gently shoved Papa back from the little door.

Papa churred impatiently. He didn't appreciate getting the cold shoulder, not when he knew Jerome was playing host to a lot of raccoons.

CHAPTER THIRTEEN

AS JEROME had expected, Emma Lou arrived before Donald got there. It was part of his plan that she should get there first. He had done a lot of planning and scheming as well as cooking. Emma Lou breezed in more like her old self than she had been for some time.

"If we can just teach the skunks and the raccoons some manners," he said. He had to start right in because Donald might come early too.

"We can teach them manners," Emma Lou said. "If they haven't been spoiled." She tossed her head.

Jerome pretended not to understand. "If we can get it through their heads that they are our guests and are not supposed to pick fights. Keeping the little skunks locked out may give them a hint."

"They're all smart," Emma Lou said.

"And they act like they owned the place," Jerome said. "Those raccoons have taken over."

Emma Lou laughed. "That's because you're an easy mark for designing brutes."

"Well, I'm the host; they're the guests. They have to be polite to one another," Jerome said gravely.

"Once they catch on, they'll be nice to each other." Emma Lou was sure. "All we have to do is to show them."

"I believe you can handle it," Jerome said. "I haven't felt up to tackling it."

"People fight, too, so you can't blame animals."

Jerome grinned. Things were shaping up pretty good. "People don't fight when they come to visit someone," he said.

"Of course they all live here," Emma Lou pointed out.

"Just the same, they're guests," Jerome insisted. He thought he had planted an idea.

Emma Lou was setting the table when Donald arrived. Not expecting her to be there, he burst into the cabin and almost knocked her over. They stood staring at each other. Emma Lou was the first to speak.

"You," she said.

"Sure it's me," Donald said. He was blushing, but he managed to grin at her.

"Well, well," Jerome broke in on them. "Just in time for supper, Donald."

They both looked at Jerome. Emma Lou's cheeks were beginning to show pink color. There was a look of understanding forming on Donald's face. Emma Lou set the sugar bowl down on the table with a thump.

Jerome cleared his throat. Right here was where his scheme would or wouldn't work. He'd know in a minute. If he could just think of something helpful to say. But he couldn't think of a thing; he just stood grinning at them.

Donald had a burlap sack in his hand. He said, "Brought some green corn. Ma will skin me when the cook tells her I snitched it."

Emma Lou's chin came up. She said coldly, "I don't see why she should be surprised."

"Not surprised, mad," Donald said.

The raccoons had smelled the green corn ears. They were crowding around Donald, jumping up at the sack. They were making a lot of noise.

"Don't stand there making them suffer," Emma Lou snapped.

Donald thrust the sack at her. He turned toward the door. Jerome got there first. "I need both of you to help me," he said firmly.

Donald looked at the girl. She was on the floor with raccoons all over her, and she was trying to shuck an ear of corn. She had one foot on the sack to keep the raccoons from dragging the ears out of it. One hand had to be used to brush raccoons away. She had to use her teeth to pull the husks loose.

"See what I mean?" Jerome said.

Donald grinned. "Well," he said slowly, "I guess I can stand it."

He sat down beside Emma Lou and began gathering in raccoons. Emma Lou shucked an ear and broke it into pieces. She passed them out, but they didn't go around. When she reached into the sack she brought out two ears. Donald accepted one, and they went to work.

Jerome crossed to the oven. He opened the door. The roast was browning nicely. He started getting things on the table. He didn't mind the silence between the two on the floor. Every once in a while he stole a glance at them. They were having so much fun feeding the raccoons that they were not thinking about how much they didn't like each other. Jerome whipped up a bowl of brown gravy, then he mashed the potatoes.

"Supper's ready," he announced. He made his way carefully to the table. There wasn't much room to move, with the raccoons ducking about trying to find safe places where they could sit and enjoy their corn.

As soon as they were seated and the plates were filled Jerome got into the subject he wanted to talk about. "Looks to me like one of us ought to have some ideas about what's to be done with the raccoons and the skunks." Jerome got a slice of roast squared around on his plate and poised his knife over it. "Donald says he has an idea, but he hasn't told me what it is."

Emma Lou helped herself to butter. "What's your bright idea?" she asked. It was the first time Jerome had ever heard her speak a civil word to Donald.

"It's just an idea so far, but it could work," Donald said eagerly.

"It better be good, and it better not be mean," Emma Lou said.

"No reason why I should spill it yet. I don't have it all worked out." When Emma Lou glared at him he grinned at her.

"I suppose you're going to sell their skins to a fur house," she said.

"That was Ben's idea; mine is better." He filled his mouth with mashed potatoes.

"And Ben got a good swift kick on the shins for that idea," Emma Lou retorted, then she grinned at Donald. "He was going to spank me for kicking him, but Amby took him down and sat on him."

Donald laughed. "I'll bet that was a battle worth seeing."

"It took Amby twenty minutes by Job's watch. But once Amby sets his mind to something, he finishes it."

Emma Lou popped a little pickled onion into her mouth.

Jerome chuckled much like one of the raccoons nibbling the milky kernels of corn. Emma Lou and Donald kept digging at one another all through supper, but anyone could see they were not angry; they were having fun. They argued fiercely about deer hunting. Emma Lou said there should be no open season at all. Donald thought it should be twice as long as it was.

"How would you like to be shot through the stomach?" she demanded.

"I'm not a buck deer," Donald argued. "Buck deer are supposed to be shot. What good are they except for venison?"

"What good are you?"

"Not much," Donald admitted. "Your brothers think the season should be open all the time." He knew this barb would hit a tender spot.

Emma Lou flushed. It was all right for one Eppy to say almost anything about another Eppy, but it wasn't all right for a Cabot to say things about an Eppy. But she was stumped for an answer that she could make fast.

Donald pointed to the roast. "I suppose that grew on a tree?"

"Men always get nasty when they argue," Emma Lou said loftily, then she added, "How did you like the venison you had last week?"

Donald didn't bat an eye. "It was swell. We had it baked with Spanish sauce. Ben's recipe."

Emma Lou almost said he would get himself grabbed by Jim Hinkle if he let Ben lead him on, but she didn't say it. "You better lay off Monarch," she said.

Jerome put in a mild word. "Looks like one part of the world was made to eat the other part. The little skunks eat mice; the raccoons eat frogs and fish."

Emma Lou looked at Jerome. She decided she had better change the subject if they were both going to argue against her. Jerome sat back and lighted his pipe. Emma Lou and Donald got going on the circus idea. Jerome listened, but he didn't pay much attention to what they were saying. He had fancied himself a philosopher when he moved into his house. He was going to be a hermit, a lazy hermit who didn't have to work or think or worry. And here he was up to his neck in other people's troubles, and facing a crisis of his own which required action and thought. He had more worries than he had ever had when he was running his shop. But he was happier, that was sure.

Emma Lou washed the dishes; Donald dried them. This arrangement was arrived at after a sharp clash of words. When Jerome's offer to do the job was unanimously refused he sat down and filled his pipe. Through a haze of blue smoke he watched them.

With the dishes washed and put away, Emma Lou lighted the fire in the fireplace. Donald appropriated Old Grouch's cushion. He didn't know it was Old Grouch's bed, and when the old raccoon walked over and sat glaring at him Donald grinned.

"He likes me," he said.

"He hates you. See the sneer on his face? You're sitting on his bed." Emma Lou giggled.

Donald moved off the cushion. He didn't want the talk to get around to Old Grouch. That might stir up a lot of things he wanted to forget. He wasn't proud of his part in the affair of the lovely lady, now that he had got to know the raccoons.

Old Grouch sniffed the cushion, then turned and ambled out through the little door which Jerome had left unlatched.

"Think the little skunks will come?" Donald asked by way of changing the subject.

"Can't say how many, but I'm sure some of them will come," Jerome said.

The raccoons were having a good time playing about on the floor. The parents joined in, and there was quite a melee of action and sounds. The little door opened and a small head poked into the room. The raccoons paid little attention when a skunk walked into the room, followed by four small skunks and another larger one.

They did not stop their romping even after three families had arrived. Jerome knew this was the moment of decision. He got up and fixed a tray of meat scraps and crumbs. Emma Lou and Donald sat watching the skunks. He was counting them.

"Seventeen," he announced when he had finished.

With the arrival of a fourth family the raccoons took notice. They had to because there were so many little skunks. They backed into a large circle and sat looking at the skunks. One baby skunk frisked over and sniffed at the nose of a baby raccoon. The raccoon playfully slapped at the little skunk. It was a very light slap, but it rolled the baby skunk over on its back. The baby squeaked and scrambled to get to its mother. Instantly eight parent skunks rushed forward. They stamped their feet and churred loudly. Jerome stood in the midst of the battle, waving his arms. But the old raccoons did not wait for matters to get out of hand. The father raccoons were the first to the little door. They zipped through fast. Then the skunks went into the final act before attack. Wildly the mother raccoons herded and shoved their children out through the door. When the last ringed tail had vanished, the eight skunks sat up and grinned at Jerome.

Jerome sank into a chair. He got out a handkerchief and mopped his forehead. Donald and Emma Lou broke into gales of laughter. Finally Donald said:

"That settles the first problem. The skunks just run the raccoons out and take over."

"There could be accidents," Jerome argued. "Suppose two of the big raccoons decided to go through the door at the same time and got stuck?" He sighed deeply. "The ones inside would go wild, and the place would be a mess."

Donald remembered the way Strong Heart had smelled after tackling one skunk. He had to agree there was danger.

"How about that plan you're working on? Having them all get along together is only part of Jerome's problem." Emma Lou intended getting the secret out of Donald if she could.

Donald leaned back and locked his hands over his knees. "It may not work," he said. He knew Emma Lou was burning up with curiosity. "It's just an idea I got one night."

"It probably won't work," Emma Lou agreed. "But you can tell us what it is."

Jerome had filled three saucers with canned milk. He set them on the floor. The parents set to work teaching the babies how to drink out of a saucer. When Jerome was seated again Donald said:

"Of course you'd have to agree to this plan."

Jerome nodded. He was a desperate man and willing

to clutch at any straw, anything short of hurting his friends. Emma Lou tossed her head impatiently.

"My dad takes half a dozen sporting magazines. You see plenty of ads offering animals for sale, wild animals and birds."

"You advertised our raccoons and skunks for sale?" Emma Lou started to bristle.

"No. I just said that anyone who would pay the shipping charges on a pair of raccoons or a pair of spotted skunks could have a pair with young ones. I said we were only interested in people who wanted to replenish the wild life of their region. No offers accepted from hunting clubs or game farms, and we'd investigate all who asked for stock." Donald paused. When he told it, it didn't sound as good as when he first thought about it.

"That is a wonderful idea," Jerome said.

"Think anyone will answer an ad like that?" Emma Lou was trying hard not to be too excited over the idea.

"I don't know," Donald said. "It's too soon for answers yet, but my dad thinks it's a grand idea. He paid for all of the ads. I was only going to run one, but he sent in three."

"How could we ship a family of skunks?" Jerome asked.

Donald grinned. "That had me worried. I wrote to a fur farm and to a zoo. It can be done."

For once Emma Lou didn't offer an argument. "You did a lot of work," she admitted. "And you did come up with an idea."

That made Donald squirm. If she had lit into him he would have liked it better. "Oh well," he said. "It wasn't much, and it may not work out."

"It's brilliant," Emma Lou said.

Jerome grinned broadly. His plan had worked out. He had patched up the quarrel. Donald was really fussed, but he liked to have Emma Lou praise him. He looked down at his boots.

"How about your skunk trick?" he asked very quickly.

Emma Lou got the seven cylinders she had used before the skunks stopped doing their trick to raise families. She got a pencil and some meat scraps. Four of the skunks knew what to do. As soon as she started tapping with her pencil they hopped upon the cylinders and started turning their heads to follow the rubber tip of the pencil. The baby skunks almost spoiled the act. They tried to get on the cylinders too. As soon as the scraps of meat were gone the parents began to look toward the door. They frisked away, with their little ones trotting behind them.

"Great show," Donald said.

Emma Lou beamed. Jerome put two more logs on the

fire. He got out the corn popper and a can of popcorn. They took over the popping. Before the corn in the first popper had stopped exploding, the raccoons were back. They sat around the hearth and sniffed eagerly. Jerome melted butter, and they had bowls of buttered corn. Donald popped two extra poppers of corn so there would be some for the raccoons. Jerome insisted upon buttering their share.

The clock on the mantel said nine. Emma Lou got to her feet. "I have to go," she said. "I promised Cilly I'd be in by nine-thirty."

"That trail is dangerous after dark," Donald said. "I have my big flashlight. I'll walk down with you."

Jerome nodded his approval. He knew Emma Lou could make the trail in the dark; she had done it a hundred times. Emma Lou hesitated just a moment, then she said:

"I forgot my flashlight."

Jerome saw them to the door. He stood in the doorway and watched the flashlight beam dance across the meadow as they headed toward the trail. After a bit he fumbled in his pocket and got out his pipe. Turning back to his fire he sat for an hour smoking and drowsing.

CHAPTER FOURTEEN

TWO WEEKS had passed and nothing had come of the ads that Donald had placed in the sporting magazines. The strain was beginning to tell.

Jerome sighed deeply as he sank into a chair beside the window. He was worn to a frazzle; his nerves were jumpy; he knew he was licked unless a miracle happened. Every night he had to face a crisis. The last skunk family was able to be out from under the house. Jerome had counted them. There were twenty-seven skunks. Papa and Mama had a new family, four husky little ones. They were very proud of the four youngsters, and they were very proud of their grandchildren.

Every night the act was the same. The skunks would come in for their milk and meat scraps. They would put the raccoons to rout after a terrific show, eat their meal, play awhile in the house, then go off for a night's romp in the woods. Sometimes Jerome felt the little skunks were all bluff, then one of them would seem really angry. Old Grouch wasn't taking the nightly insult very well. Twice he had come very near tangling with Papa. Runt was always egging her husband on, trying to get him to stand up to the skunks. So far he had not showed much willingness to be firm, but Jerome knew Runt was smart. She usually got her way. Last night the burly one had made a lot of noise before charging out through the little door. Tonight he might wade into the skunks.

Emma Lou and Donald had buried the war hatchet, though not very deep. That gave Jerome some consolation. They argued often and with much heat, but their friendship seemed well established. No answers had come in from the magazine ads, but they did not seem worried. They had great fun with the raccoons and the skunks. Donald always enjoyed the nightly rout of the raccoons. Jerome had an idea they didn't want to see them sent away.

By way of being ready Jerome had put a wall and a door on the shed Monarch had used. He made the shed raccoon- and skunk-proof. He cleaned it out and fixed some blankets on a pine-bough bed in a corner. He built shelves against one wall and stored canned food and extra clothing and his strongbox in the little shed. In case of trouble he would have a place of refuge. The wood mice soon discovered this skunk-proof house and made it a place of sanctuary. As always happens with mice, they set up housekeeping at once and soon had downy nests in the boughs piled up for a bed, and in back of the cans on the shelves. One pair built their nest inside one of the boots Jerome had stored in a box. If he had to move into the little shed Jerome would not be without company.

It was Saturday. The house needed cleaning, but Jerome didn't feel up to scrubbing the floor. He leaned back and elevated his feet to the table top. He was about to close his eyes when he saw Emma Lou coming across the meadow. He remembered she had promised to help with the house cleaning. He wasn't going to get his nap. She would start right in scrubbing and cleaning.

She came in with a cheery hello. Jerome smiled at her. It was a weak smile, the smile of a man who is beaten and knows he is beaten.

"We'll give this place a real going over," Emma Lou said cheerfully. She began whistling as she started dumping raccoons out of the boxes scattered around the room. The raccoons did not like being roused from their warm and comfortable beds. They liked it less when she shooed them outside with the broom. She set their boxes out in the sun.

Jerome stirred himself. The house needed a good cleaning. There was more than a faint raccoon smell, and there was just a trace of skunk smell. He built a fire and got a tub of water on to heat. They were about ready to start scrubbing the floor when Donald arrived. He was red-faced and out of breath from running uphill. He was waving a sheaf of letters.

"They came!" he shouted.

CHAPTER FOURTEEN

Jerome dropped the mop, and Emma Lou tossed aside the broom. She dashed to meet him. Jerome just stood with his mouth open.

"The plan worked?" Emma Lou asked eagerly.

"Did it! Say, we're about to make history." He was

waving the letters. Emma Lou was trying to get hold of them. "We've done something big."

"Don't stand there. What is it?" Emma Lou shouted.

"The skunks. You should see the letters about the spotted skunks. Why, Jerome's spotted skunks are rare animals, about extinct. A dozen zoos want them, and four big estates want them. We won't have enough to go around."

"Honest?" Emma Lou's eyes were shining.

"Read 'em." Donald tossed the letters on the table. "We have places for all the raccoons, too."

Jerome sank into a chair beside the table. He pulled a letter toward him and began reading it. Emma Lou sat across from him. She started reading letters. When they had read all of them she looked across at Jerome.

"You won't send them all away?" she asked anxiously.

"No," he said. "I'll keep Papa and Mama and Old Grouch."

"They'll even come here and get the little skunks," Donald said.

"We have to check carefully to make sure there are no fur farmers," Emma Lou said.

Donald grinned. "Dad likes our idea. He'll check up on everyone through his office."

"Well," Jerome said. Then he repeated, "Well."

"It's wonderful," Emma Lou burst out. She was looking at Donald when she said it. His face got red.

"Nuts," he said. Then he grinned at Emma Lou.